Tricks of the Trade

The unseen rifleman fired again and this time Stringer knew for sure who the intended target was. It was not the demented longhorn. So Stringer drew his six-gun and hung down the far side of his mount, Comanche style, as he rode for the bush cover.

It almost worked. They were most of the way down the slope when Stringer felt the wet smack of his mount taking a rifle round and let go the horn to land running as the old bay dove ass-over-tea-kettle into some sunflower stalks and just lay there . . .

LOU CAMERON

STRINGER

AND THE OIL WELL INDIANS

CHARTER BOOKS, NEW YORK

STRINGER AND THE OIL WELL INDIANS

A Charter Book/published by arrangement with
the author

PRINTING HISTORY
Charter edition/February 1989

ISBN: 1-55773-161-6

Charter Books are published by The Berkley Publishing Group,
200 Madison Avenue, New York, N.Y. 10016.
The name "Charter" and the "C" logo are trademarks belonging
to Charter Communications Inc.

PRINTED IN THE UNITED STATES OF AMERICA

10 9 8 7 6 5 4 3 2 1

CHAPTER
ONE

The first thing Stringer noticed about Tulsa was that he seemed overdressed for the occasion. Recalling the erstwhile flag stop of Creek City as a cow town, he'd dropped off the night train in faded but clean blue denims and a reasonably clean Rough Rider hat that was supposed to be pearl gray. But the planks of the railroad platform were coated with sticky black rock-oil and a mist of the same stinky stuff was descending on him from the sullen red midnight sky. So he ran with his gladstone bag for the shelter of the depot waiting room, lest he wind up looking like that tar baby in the Uncle Remus stories.

As he braced his already greasy gladstone on a bench to get at his yellow rain slicker, an older gent puffing a pipe across the aisle chuckled and said, "Great minds run in the same channels. Old Blackjack Sinclair just brung in another gusher up to the west end of town.

1

Won't be a fit night out for man nor beast until they cap the son of a bitch with a Christmas tree."

He spat and added, morosely, "I wish they wouldn't drill right here in town, don't you?"

Stringer didn't answer until he'd slipped into his slicker. Then he opined rock-oil sure smelled disgusting. As the old-timer allowed there was money in stink, if you had enough of it to sell, Stringer considered the S&W .38 reposing in its coiled gun rig atop his other possibles. The Indian Nation had been rough country in its day, he knew. But, hell, a new century had dawned and they were calling it the Oklahoma Territory these days. He'd been sent to do a feature on the spanking new rock-oil industry, not to start a war, so he proceeded to shut the lid on his old six-gun, and would have, had not the streetside door crashed open to admit a burly black figure with a .45 in each hand and a string of curses already blasting from its lips.

Since Stringer heard his own name braided in with "Nosy son of a bitch!" and "Meddling motherfucker!" he naturally dove to the floor and rolled under the bench with the gun from his own open bag, just as the greasy gunslick in the doorway got down to tearing slivers from the backrest of the bench with a fusillade of flying slugs. Blinded by his own gunsmoke in the poorly-lit waiting room, the cuss in the doorway ceased fire long enough to call out, "Where are you at? Stand up and fight like a man, you pencil-pushing sissy-boy!"

So Stringer rose, where he wasn't expected to, and put three rounds into his attacker's chest, with somewhat better aim.

The black hulk staggered back outside and the sprung doors swung shut as if nothing much had happened. A still smoking .45 that lay just inside the door told

Stringer something had. He knew better than to chase the other gun and whoever might still be holding it out *that* way. So he whirled and ran out the doorway on the platform side as, behind him, an elderly voice called wistfully, "Hey, can I come out now?"

Stringer didn't know. So he just circled the frame building until he could stick his head and gun muzzle around a streetside corner to see what he might have wrought. There were no street lamps shining at this hour. But the glowering light of the red sky above illuminated the black form near the doorway well enough for Stringer to move closer, reloading as he watched for any signs of life and failing to see any.

There were no signs of life from the man he'd just shot, but there were plenty of other black figures headed his way now, drawn to the sounds of gunplay. Stringer kicked the remaining six-gun near the dead man inside as he opened the door and followed it, calling out, "It's over, old son, and I sure hope you'll recall whose notion it was to start it."

The old timer he'd been talking to before didn't answer. He wasn't there any more. Some gents were like that when two gents they neither knowed nor owed got into a fight that could lead to all sorts of tedious questions.

So Stringer was standing alone by his open gladstone, his .38 holstered under his slicker while he rolled a smoke and waited for the inevitable.

The inevitable entered with his own gun drawn and a silver star pinned to his oily slicker. Stringer noticed the deputy had a slight but hard to place accent as he nodded in a friendly enough way and announced, "I'd be Deputy Marshal Chris Madsen. I hope you've heard of me. I don't like to brag, but it can save unfortunate moves on the parts of others if I just say my name, right out. You've heard of me, I hope?"

Stringer regarded the somewhat older and much heavier man with respect as he replied, "I've heard of you. They say you're the fastest Swede in the west."

Madsen looked pained and said, "I'll have you know I'm Danish, and I'll thank you to keep that in mind. I'm an awfully sweet-natured cuss, myself. But some Danes take being called a Swede about the way a Cherokee takes being called a Creek."

Another deputy came in the far door with his gun drawn. He said, "The yard bulls say they spotted a man crossing the tracks in one hell of a hurry, just after they heard the same shots we did. No sign of him now, and they didn't see enough of him to describe him."

Chris Madsen cocked a questioning eyebrow at Stringer, who said, "That would have been my one and only witness. I was the one as shot the gent out front. I don't know why, either. They call me Stringer MacKail. I write for the *San Francisco Sun*. My feature editor sent me to write up your new oil boom and I'd just gotten off the eastbound when that other owlhoot busted in here cussing and shooting."

Madsen frowned thoughtfully and said, "I'm tempted to buy a story that dumb. It's been my experience that folks usually premeditate an ingenious excuse as well as the murder to go with it."

The husky lawman lowered his gun muzzle to his side, but then he added, "We'd best go have a talk with my boss about it, now. Button your slicker over that .38 and we'll treat you as decent as you treat us, for now."

As Stringer did as he was told, Madsen turned to the deputy covering him from the far side and said, "You and the other boys had best see the dead man to the undertaker. Have them put him on ice until we can figure out who's burying him. Make sure you pat him down for I.D. before you report back to the lockup." Then he added, "Let's go, MacKail," and Stringer took the lead, as he knew he was supposed to.

Outside, the drizzle of rock-oil had let up. But the night was still overcast and the clouds above still glowed like flickering embers. Madsen waved his .45 indicating the direction they were headed, and said it wasn't far, adding, "I'm sure glad they capped that well at last. Blackjack Sinclair is a real pest, drilling right through an old lady's front porch like that and gushing everyone downwind without a word of warning."

As they strode up the tarry rutted street, each rut filled to overflowing with reeking rock-oil, Stringer could see by the sky glow that they were surrounded by a forest of big black oil well derricks. None of them seemed to be on fire, so he asked Madsen why the skies above glowed so red at night.

Madsen explained, "Gas flares. The oil fizzles out of the ground filled with bubbles of natural gas and they got to get rid of it somehow. There's little market for the stuff and it's too dangerous to just let it drift. As you can see, it's highly inflammable. So it's better to flame it on purpose than it is to let it catch fire by accident." Then he said, "That doorway to your right is where we're going. You go first and make sure your hands are polite as you enter. My boss, Bill Tilghman, is quicker on the draw than me and he doesn't like surprises."

Stringer could see that as he opened the door and stepped into the front office of the glorified shack. The lean and somewhat older man behind the desk set up in front of the row of holding cages rose from his seat with catlike grace and put a thoughtful hand to the grips of

his low slung six-gun. Then he spotted his deputy behind Stringer and relaxed, asking, "What have we
here?" in a calm and almost friendly voice.

Stringer knew who *he* was. Senior Deputy U.S.
Marshal William Tilghman had become a legend in his
own time. Stringer was mildly surprised but not as-
tounded to note that the man who'd cleaned up the
Cherokee Strip had a pleasant amiable face behind a
walrus moustache of steel wire suitable for scrubbing
pots and pans.

Chris Madsen introduced Stringer and told Tilghman, "He strikes me as a reasonable young cuss, considering the wild story he has to tell." So Tilghman
moved over to a nearby filing cabinet to take three hotel
tumblers and a fifth of rye from a drawer as he told
Stringer he'd just love to hear his tale.

As Stringer repeated the details of his mysterious
shoot-out to the two older lawmen, he noticed neither
Tilghman nor Madsen seemed to require as much re-
freshment as they served him. He knew better than to
ask if they were trying to get him drunk. Stringer had a
clear conscience and a Scotch stomach for hard liquor.
So all three of them were still sober as he ran out of
things to say and said so.

Bill Tilghman nodded soberly and allowed, "I've
read the stuff you write for the newspapers, MacKail.
You do lard it on a mite about events west of the Big
Muddy, no offense, but, so far, I've yet to catch you in
a total fib. Leaving your rude welcome to our fair city
aside for now, what brung you to Tulsa in the first
place?"

Stringer smiled thinly and said, "My boss, old Sam
Barca, seems to think unusual events are happening
here. He recalls what you now call Tulsa as a sleepy

little crossroads called Creek Town. I guess nobody knew there was oil under it when it grew up around an Indian trading post."

Tilghman grimaced and replied, "It was tough enough as it was. There's so-called civilized Creek to the south, Osage to the north and Cherokee to the east. All three get along better with white Sooners than one another, and now this oil boom has the usual whores, gamblers and general misfits drifting in to spice up an already simmering stew. I'd say you just met up with one of the same, if I could say who he might have been. The town law they had here gave up on trying to control Tulsa more than a week ago. That's how come me and my boys was sent over from our regular post at Perry with direct orders to hold down the noise." He took a sip from his own glass before adding, "You sure are a noisy young cuss, and I'd feel a lot better about you if that witness had come forward."

The door behind Stringer opened and the deputy he'd seen back at the depot came in to hang up his greasy slicker as he sighed and stated, "That dead son of a bitch had shit as well as rock-oil all over his damned wallet. But I done my duty. A voter's registration card he was packing says he used to be a James J. Woods from Amarillo."

Bill Tilghman grinned like a mean little kid as he told Stringer, "You're free to go, MacKail. I recall that alias from a wanted flier the Texas Rangers sent me a spell back. The real name was Jack Holt. Used to work for Pinkerton. Got fired for strike-breaking beyond the call of duty or common sense. Since then he's been in business for himself as a hired gun."

Chris Madsen blinked thoughtfully. "Wasn't Jack Holt the name we were given in connection with that pretty young Creek gal the Creeks accused the Cherokee of raping and murdering a year or so back, Bill?"

Tilghman nodded and said, "That, too. But I doubt he was out to ravage this boy's fair white body. He killed for hard cash, not pleasure." Then he cocked an eyebrow at Stringer to add, "We'd best go over it all again, old son. For a man who just arrived in Tulsa, you seem to make enemies mighty sudden."

Stringer shook his head and said, "I've already told you all I know, damn it. Save for you boys and that old man at the railroad depot I just don't *know* anyone in this town!"

Chris Madsen said, "Try it this way, then. You've a rep as a muck-racking newspaper man, no offense, and Lord knows there's a heap of muck to be raked in this neck of the woods. How do you know some slicker you exposed in the past got here ahead of you, heard you were coming, and sent Holt to head you off at that depot before you could write mean things about anyone?"

Stringer didn't answer as he ran that through his brain a time or two.

Bill Tilghman said, "I read what you wrote not long ago about them fellers selling stock in that salted silver mine. Our job is to keep the peace, not look into oil well stocks. But I can tell you there's a heap of such bullshit taking place in Tulsa these days."

Stringer shook his head and said, "I learned a little about the mining game covering the Alaska Gold Rush, right after the war with Spain. But you gents have to know more about drilling for oil than I do. I just got here. This is the first oil boom I've ever covered."

Tilghman insisted, "You mean *tried* to, don't you? Seems to me someone hired Holt to gun you before you could even have a look around. You could be overly modest. I said I'd read your stuff, and you do have a nose for flimflamming. Just what were you figuring on looking at and writing about here, starting from the top."

Stringer shrugged and said, "I arrived with an open mind. I just told you it was my first oil boom. Sam Barca told me to look for local color. The rock-oil industry is new to most of our readers as well. We'd heard back in Frisco what you just said about sudden money attracting colorful characters from all over the West, and you know how Wild West features sell."

Bill Tilghman suppressed a groan and said, "If you write any wild West bullshit about me and mine I'll sue you. That crazy Ned Buntline published a string of outright lies about me and my boys, and poor old Judge Parker, then he up and died before we could get at him. He even writ that he'd presented me with one of his Buntline Specials, and I never *met* the son of a bitch."

Stringer smiled and said, "I've heard you don't like to give interviews, sir. That's likely why you're not as famous as say, old Wyatt Earp."

Bill Tilghman scowled and said, "That piss ant's as big a liar as Ned Buntline was," and Chris Madsen chimed in, "We recall him in the Indian Nation as a horse thief. It was his elder brother, Virgil, as rid shotgun for Wells Fargo and got to wear a town deputy badge until they shot him. Old Wyatt was never no more than a tagalong kid brother."

Stringer sighed and said, "They told me much the same tale in Tombstone, last time I was there. My editor was afraid to publish my account of the O.K. Corral Fight as it really happened. Wyatt's made a lot of friends in the new moving picture game out on the West Coast and, hell, his version makes for a more exciting two-reeler. I'd sure like to take down your version of the way you, Heck Thomas, and old Bill, here, cleaned the plow of the Doolin-Dalton gang a few years back, Chris."

Madsen just look disgusted. Tilghman said, "No, you wouldn't. Them two young whores they had riding with 'em, Cattle Annie and Little Britches, already told enough lies about me and mine. It's my own fault for taking 'em in alive, soft-hearted as I am. Forget ancient history, MacKail. The question before the house, in the here and now, is who sent Jack Holt after you and what we ought to do about it."

Stringer shrugged and said, "I don't see what anyone can do about it unless and until they make their next move. I don't have even a wild guess as to who might want me dead, or why."

Bill Tilghman nodded and replied, "That's what I just said. You were lucky as hell at the depot. You owe Blackjack Sinclair your life. If he hadn't brought in that gusher just before you arrived, you'd have doubtless strode straight for Main Street with your own gun packed away in your gladstone, like you said. Holt must have been waiting for you in the open when you both started to get lubricated from on high. Running through that mist of rock-oil must have made that hired gun so mad he wasn't able to approach you with a cool head and sneaky smile. So you won that time. The *next* one they send after you will know you ain't a gent to be treated so careless, and you won't know him at all as he comes sidewinding your way. So, if I was you, I'd hop the next train out. As things stand now, your future here in Tulsa figures to be fatal. You'd best stay here with us until the next train pulls in around four in the morning. We can likely put you on board safe and sound, see?"

Stringer shook his head and said, "I don't run out of town that easy, even when I know who wants me out of town. I'm paid to write about such doings, not run from them. But since you're so interested in my comfort, could you point me at a decent hotel, assuming I'm not under arrest anymore?"

Bill Tilghman sighed and said, "You sure must get paid a lot more than I do. I've backed out of saloons for less reason than this and I'm not ashamed to say so. That's how I got to be so much older and wiser than you."

Chris Madsen said, "The Osage Inn down the street is as decent a hotel as you can get to from here without a cavalry troop covering your back. Do you want me to walk him over there, Bill?"

Tilghman nodded and said, "Take a couple of the boys with you and see if you can't talk some sense into him along the way."

Madsen nodded and took a ten-gauge shotgun from the gun rack near the door as Tilghman told Stringer, "We'll be proud to hang anyone who back-shoots you, provided we catch him. But we have better things to do than ride herd on a wayward youth who just won't pay attention to his elders. Once you kiss old Chris good-night, you'll be on your own, you poor stubborn sap."

CHAPTER
TWO

The small lobby of the Osage Inn was naturally empty at this hour. The threadbare rug and potted rubber plants looked clean enough, despite the eye-watering smell. As he paid the clerk behind the counter an outrageous dollar for the hire of one tiny room, Stringer asked suspiciously if they'd been spraying for bugs.

The sleepy-eyed clerk replied stiffly, "We don't allow bugs, or even Creeks to stay in this establishment, Mister, ah, MacKail. That reek is coming in from outside. The whole damned town has got to stinking like a cheesebox-still since they drilled all them oil wells in ever' direction. I can see by your slicker you was out in the deluge when Blackjack Sinclair sunk that last one just up the street."

Stringer nodded and said, "They've capped it, whatever that means. What do you boys do about such crud on your hats, between oil storms?"

The clerk handed over the room key as he replied, "Dunking 'em in white naptha helps. But it's best to have two hats in Tulsa these days. They hardly ever bring in a gusher on Sunday, when you need to get presenticated for Church. The rest of the time we just pretend a greasy hat is the lastest fashion. I used to have a bellhop around here. I reckon the fool kid ran up the street to watch 'em cap that last strike. You'd think he'd have gotten used to that by now. But you know how kids are."

Stringer said he'd been a kid one time and that he could tote one bag if he really put his mind to it. He went up the stairwell to the third floor room that matched the number on his key tag and saw the hallway was dimly illuminated by forty watt Edison bulbs. He was glad. He'd already decided to give up smoking until the natural gas in the air all about him cleared away or blew up the whole town.

The corner room he'd hired seemed clean enough but smelled like the inside of an oil lamp. He put his slicker and gladstone in the well-greased closet and switched off the lamp by the brass bedstead before he raised the blinds and threw open the windows for some cross ventilation. It didn't help much. But from up here he had his first clear view across the lower rooftops all around.

Gas flares, birthday-caked all over town, outlined the black open timberwork of five-story drilling derricks closer in. One just up the street loomed a lot closer and its coat of inky oil shone like fresh stove blacking. He knew he owed that derrick the polka dots all over his poor hat, and likely his life as well. He told himself it was way past bedtime and that a man with a lick of sense called it a day while he was still ahead, but he was too keyed-up to consider counting sheep, and he knew that hired guns tended to work in bunches or solo. Had the late Jack Holt come at him as part of a bunch, it hardly seemed likely he'd be having this fool conversation with himself. So the dimly lit streets of Tulsa were likely as safe right now as they were apt to be at any future time and, Hell, he was as curious about late night fire engines, wasn't he?

Stringer stepped out in the hall and locked the door. Then he pocketed the key and moved quietly down the stairs. As he'd hoped, there was a fire exit at the foot of the stairs that opened into a side alley. So he left the Osage Inn by that route lest he disturb the room clerk or attract the notice of anyone more ferocious.

He moved up toward the new well trying to keep to the shadows. There were lots of them with all the shops closed and shuttered for the night, and the sullen red sky-glow blocked by many plank awnings. As he made out the crowd around the base of the new derrick he saw that it rose like a steeple from a bitty frame house that might have been most any color before its recent coat of still-wet crude. The drilling platform of the dripping derrick spread from the front steps of the little house out to the street and then some. As Stringer drifted quietly into the clumps of roughnecks and rubber-neckers clustered around the base of the derrick nobody seemed to notice him. He reached absently for the Bull Durham tag dangling from his shirt pocket, decided that smoking right then could be injurious to his health, and studied the confused clutter between the four massive legs of the derrick as he tried to fathom the mysterious rites of the new industry.

Roping a stray in chaparral seemed less complicated. But it was easy enough to see why they called the confusion of pipes and valves now rising from the center of

the platform a Christmas tree. It almost resembled a
bare-branched pine of pipe with brass valve wheels and
dials decorating every branch. A thick black firehose of
rubber or tar-coated canvas ran from a stub at the base
of the contraption to snake over the edge of the platform
and vanish around one corner of the oil-soaked little
house. He'd just assured himself that was where the oil
that had showered him earlier had to be going, and that
the business wasn't all that mysterious, after all, when
one of the derrick hands spoiled it all by asking another,
"Don't you think we should bleed some gas, Tiger? The
pressure gauge is in the red and that hose ain't as young
as it used to be."

The one who figured to be the straw boss, a husky
giant in oil-coated overalls and an oilcloth fisherman's
hat, told his worried assistant to let *him* do the worrying
and added, "The hose will split afore the cap will go.
There's already too much gas in the air here for a man to
breathe right."

The smaller roughneck sighed and said, "I noticed. A
lot more gas figures to spew out anywhere the damned
hose splits and it stretches half a mile through all sorts
of back yards, Tiger."

But Tiger, as he no doubt enjoyed being called, just
shrugged and said, "Better them than us. It'd be cheaper
to replace a shack full of trash Indians than it would be
to replace this rig or my poor white ass. Crack the wet-
valve a quarter turn and see if that don't ease the pressure a mite. Touch the gas bleeder and if the gas don't
kill you, I will."

The lesser mortal climbed back up to fool with the
Christmas tree. Stringer stared at the block and tackle
dangling loose above the workman and the valves he
was working on, trying to figure out why all that wire

cable was just dangling. Before he could spot anyone in the crowd who looked both amiable and up on the subject, the front door of the oil-soaked house popped open and a tall thin gent dressed dapper above the knees and wearing oily rubber boots from there down came out packing a briefcase and an expression of extreme disgust as he approached the one called Tiger, saying, "Well, the signatures I just got might stand up in court. Then, again, they might not. Whatever could have possessed you to drill without a proper permit from the owner of the property, damn it?"

Tiger shrugged and said, "Hell, the old lady inside told us it was jake with her, as soon as the boss told her how rich a lady with an oil well in her front yard was likely to wind up. You know the boss holds it to be a scientifical fact that blackjack oak grows mostly over oil domes and there was a blackjack sapling growing in her garden afore we cut it down to lay out our platform. What was we supposed to do, let Standard Oil make her a better offer whilst you lawyers was dotting every I and crossing every T?"

The lawyer held his briefcase higher, like a trophy, and snapped, "That's exactly what I expect you to do, next time. Oral permission or even written permission from the likes of that old squaw is worthless. Lucky for Sinclair Oil, her son-in-law is a breed, living off the B.I.A. Rolls and thus, not a ward of the government, as Indian as he may look. I just got him to sign the lease for the family, at two cents a barrel more than I might have had to if he hadn't been white enough to see he had us by the nuts, with the well already proven, and not so much as an X in crayon on paper!"

Tiger shrugged his massive shoulders and said, "I just drill for the stuff, Mister Lacey. Take it up with

Mister Sinclair if you don't cotton to my style."

The lawyer said stiffly, "I just told you I'd covered your mistake. Nobody said anything about firing you, damn it."

Tiger smiled smugly and replied, "I don't much care if you do. I ain't one for bragging, but we both know how many other outfits are drilling out there, right now, and that I'm the best damned driller in the game."

The lawyer smiled thinly and said, "Well, you're about as *fast* a driller as we've ever had. But try to keep it in mind that this is a business, not a gopher race. A well tied up in federal court can be less profitable than one on *fire*! At least we can insure a rig against fire. These damned conflicting Indian claims mean we really *have* to dot every I and cross every T before we even cut down a tree. So don't do that again and we'll say no more about it."

Then the lawyer was looking Stringer's way, not too pleasantly. Stringer looked somewhere else and faded casually back from the crowd. He'd heard as much or more about the local situation than the prissy Lawyer Lacey was likely to tell him, and Stringer just wasn't up to stating his own name and business to strangers again. He suspected he might already be known in Tulsa by more than enough mean-eyed gents.

It had to be pushing two A.M. by now, and that big brass bedstead had cost him a whole silver dollar, so he wandered back to his hotel. He entered by the same side door, having wedged it open when he'd left, and the stairs did seem a mite steeper now, as he went back up to his room.

He's just shut the door behind him when someone commenced to tap it softly from the other side. Stringer doubted it could be a raven softly rapping on his chamber door, so he drew his S&W as he cracked it open. Then he blinked in pleased surprise and asked the perky little blonde in the red kimono, "What on earth are you doing in Tulsa, Bubbles?"

W.R. Hackman, as she bylined the features she wrote for the *Los Angeles Examiner*, told Stringer that was what she wanted to ask *him* as she pushed her way in and shut the hall door behind her little round rump. Stringer saw no need to flick the light switch on. He could see her curves pretty well by the ruby glow through the windows and he could picture any details he might be missing from memory, thanks to the all-too-short, but mighty sweet time they'd shacked up in Tombstone. He put his gun back in its holster and reeled in the pretty little newspaper gal for a not at all brotherly kiss. She kissed back just as warmly, with a French accent. Then she pulled halfway free of his embrace to demand, "Aren't we taking a lot for granted, Mister MacKail?"

He shrugged and replied, "If you say so. I didn't know this was a purely business call, Ma'am. My paper sent me to do a piece on this Oklahoma oil boom. I'm hardly stupid enough to ask if the *Examiner* sent you to write about wild Indians."

She dimpled up at him and said, "As a matter of fact, they did. It's the first time anyone's struck oil under an Indian reservation. Do you think they're going to get cheated out of this otherwise worthless land, now that it's *worth* something?"

He said, "I just heard a lawyer discussing that subject. Just what are we discussing, W.R.? Shared coverage, like that time in Tombstone?"

She wrinkled her pert nose as she answered, "As I recall, you kept kicking the covers off, and it gets cold at night in Arizona. Do you suppose it might be remotely possible this time, to keep our shared news angles on a more professional basis? I told you when we parted, that last cold gray dawn, that I just wasn't up to feeling loved and left."

Stringer smiled down at her wistfully and told her, "Cold gray dawns are uncomfortable for me, too. You may be right. It may be best if, this time, we work separate. You know how weak-natured I am when it comes to, ah, comparing notes with such a nice-looking member of the Fourth Estate and, to tell the truth, I don't know beans about oil wells."

She asked, "What about Indians?" to which he could only answer, "The Trail Of Tears was before my time, and it's my understanding the Civilized Tribes were living white before Andrew Jackson drove 'em out here. The Cherokee, Chickashas, Choctaws, Creeks and Seminole were eastern woodland nations who'd taken to raising cash crops and acting about like everyone else before Old Hickory decided their farms and businesses were too good for anyone but whites who voted for him regular. The Osage were Sioux-speaking plainsmen who took up civilization as soon as they saw how well the Cherokee and Creek were doing, living white. The Indians in this particular neck of the woods are Creek, Osage and Cherokee. Most of 'em are part white, this late in the game, and a mess of white Sooners have moved in since the old Indian Nation was made the Oklahoma Territory and opened to homesteading wherever Indians weren't already settled. Can we talk about it in the morning? It's late as hell and I'm just not up to giving history lectures at this infernal hour."

She started to say something. Then she sighed and moved over to the bedstead. As she slipped out of her kimono to recline crossways on the bed covers, Stringer smiled crookedly and asked her, "Is that your notion of a strictly business relationship, Bubbles?"

To which she replied, demurely, "If you offer to pay me I'll snatch you bald-headed. You might have put up more of an argument, you brute!"

But all seemed forgiven by the time Stringer had shucked his own duds to the floor, hung his hat and gun-rig over a bed post, and joined her atop the covers to get nice and warm.

He'd forgotten just how warm old W.R. could get, for like the memories of pain, the memories of pleasure tended to blur as soon as one got over them. But it began to feel like old times in the Promised Land as they went gloriously insane together for a spell. But, when they had to pause for their second wind and Stringer decided the air had cleared enough now to risk lighting a smoke, he saw by the flickering matchlight that she had tears running down both cheeks from her big blue eyes. He shook out the match and cuddled her closer with his free arm, soothing, "You should have told me if I was hurting you, honey."

She sobbed, "Oh, shut up. You know I came ahead of you, and damn it, the magic has started again and I made up my mind the last time, that a girl with a, well, adventurous streak had no call to take a tumbleweed man like you so seriously. Why can't I just enjoy it, as good dirty fun, the way *you* do?"

He patted her bare shoulder to comfort her as he suggested, "Maybe it's because you're not as big and mean as me. I wasn't having dirty thoughts about you just now, Bubbles. If anything, I was all too aware I was violating Teddy Roosevelt's new pure food acts, you pretty little slice of angel's food cake."

She snuggled closer but got tears all over his bare chest as she protested, "I was trying to enjoy it as just fun. I'm sorry I moaned all those love words at you as I was coming. You must think I'm an awful sissy, right?"

He kissed the part of her unbound hair and assured her, "Hell, gals have a right to sound sissy, even when they *ain't* coming. If you'll promise not to print it in your paper, I'll confess I was sure I was in love with you, too, when you bit down so sweet with your innards at the last."

She brightened and asked, "Want to see me do it again?" So he put out the cigarette he'd just lit and although he felt a lot more than he could see, she sure could crunch down on an exploding erection with her already tight little organ grinder. She did it even better on top, and the ruby light gleaming on her parts that had inspired him to name her Bubbles inspired him to finish right, with her on the bottom, her ankles locked lovingly around the nape of his neck.

It seemed to calm her down instead of making her cry that time. Stringer was having enough trouble with his breathing without a smoke. So they just lay cuddled like old pards for a spell. Then she said she was getting goose bumps from the cold night air and they got under the covers together, lined up with the bed springs, with their heads on the pillows, and that inspired them to squeak the springs some more with one of the pillows under her already well-padded derriere. She said she found it a new and novel position. She'd told him that time in Tombstone that she'd never been married to a missionary. He'd never asked and still didn't want to know who'd taught her all those other novel positions and when they'd finished this time, she said she was really tired and asked if he hadn't had enough for now.

He kissed her, laughed, and replied, "It depends on what parts of me you're asking. I'll allow my back is tired of you for the moment. I had a long day on a hardwood train seat and the night wasn't all that restful, either. Before I met up with you again, I mean."

She stiffened slightly to ask, "Oh? Just who might you have met that thrilled you so, before I heard you were staying at the same hotel, you sex fiend?"

He chuckled fondly and said, "If you think I could do what I just done to two women in one night, you really must admire me. My previous excitement was with a hired gun named Jack Holt. I've found such encounters almost as exciting as sex, even when I win. Who told you I was staying here at the Osage Inn, speaking of exciting encounters?"

She said, "I'm not deaf and the depot's only a city block from here. But even a newswoman has to slip something on before she covers a shoot-out and you'd left by the time I was on the scene. One of the lawmen scraping up the mess you'd left told me the winner had been a young cowboy named MacKail. So after I wrote the item up and wired it in, I came back here to coyly inquire whether anyone by that name might have checked into the only decent hotel for blocks. By the time I could make myself, ah, presentable, you'd left again, you fidgety thing. I was just about to fall asleep when I heard familiar footsteps in the hall. Why do you always wear spurs, darling?"

He said, "I don't have 'em on right now. The rest of the time it's too big a bother to get 'em on and off right, and a man just never knows when he may want to ride, a horse, I mean."

She said, "I've only seen a few cowboys, or Indians dressed like cowboys, since I got here around noon. But

I'm glad you clunked by my door in those spurred boots of yours. I'm sort of weak-natured, too."

He said, "I noticed how you make yourself presentable to tell a man not to trifle with you. I don't think we have to worry about waking up in any cold gray dawn, at the rate we're going. But we're going to have to study some on just how close we want to stick when we wake up at, oh, say, noon."

She propped herself up on one elbow, resting a bare breast where her head had just been, to demand, "Just what do you mean by that, MacKail? I thought we just agreed to cover the story together, like we did that time in Tombstone."

He hauled her back down and said soothingly, "The shooting was over that time, by the time we wound up sharing notes and kisses. I don't know what the story might *be* here in Tulsa, and the shooting may have just started. I'm not trying to get rid of you, Bubbles. I'm just out to keep you alive. The two of us can dig up more news, separate, without exposing you to the danger of my company in public, see?"

She didn't. She said, "Pooh, I still pack a ladylike little pistol in my purse and I'll thank you to remember how happy you were about *that* when that rascal in Tombstone had the drop on you. The two of us make a dangerous team to tangle with and, in any case, a reporter is a reporter when someone has something to hide behind a hired gun."

He nodded but said, "I'm not sure Holt was sent to hide a thing here in Tulsa. I don't know anyone here but the law, and while lawmen have been known to bend the rules, the breed of tough old birds policing this town don't *need* to hire guns. On the other hand, I have made enemies all over in my travels. I was covering a water works scandal out on the coast just before Sam Barca sent me here. Crooked contractors might not *know* my boss just won't run exposés on crooks who run full page ads in *The Sun*."

She thought before she decided, "Crooks here in Tulsa make more sense, dear. Frisco big shots could get you fired just as easy as they could have you killed. Those crooks in Tombstone never went after me or any other reporter but you, remember? It was you who exposed that salted silver mine, just as they'd feared you might. You have a rep for spotting crooked mining deals and, well, isn't rock-oil a mineral?"

He laughed incredulously and replied, "Not any kind of mineral I know beans about, Bubbles. I just had a look at an oil well and I still don't savvy what I was looking at. I grew up in gold mining country and I was lucky enough to sniff salt when I was covering the Alaska Rush a few years ago. Once you know just a mite about hardrock mining your nose sort of twitches when things don't smell right. I spotted those swindlers in Tombstone just because they seemed to be going about silver mining the wrong way. I don't *know* the way you drill for rock-oil. Aside from that, I don't think there's any way to fake one. You just drill down until you strike oil or don't. I've heard of crooks selling stock and not drilling at all. But . . ."

"You see?" she cut in, "You've already thought of a way to crook people with fake oil stock, just like those crooks were doing with silver stock in Tombstone that time! I'll bet that's what some crooks here in Tulsa are worried about!"

He started to tell her not to be silly. Then he said, more thoughtfully, "I don't see how anyone could be worried about me spotting an oil derrick that ain't here.

Oil stocks are peddled back east, on Wall Street, as I understand the game. I don't think my boss would spring for train fare to New York City and even if he did, I'd be lost as a babe in the woods amidst all that ticker tape. Even if I was able to make heads or tails of the stock market, why would a confidence man back east want to have me gunned out west? That water works scandal I was digging into works as well, or better."

She insisted, "Don't be so modest. You said you just got here and barely knew anything about oil wells. There's a forest of them growing, just outside, and if even only one of them is being run crooked, knowing you were poking about could make a crook nervous as anything. Don't you remember that you didn't *know* that silver mine in Tombstone was being operated by crooks until they shot at you to keep you from finding out, and made you find out?"

He yawned and said, "Maybe. Right now we're just talking in circles and, no offense, I don't feel up to talking any more about oil wells, right now."

So she said, "Goody. Neither do I. Isn't it my turn to get on top, this time?"

CHAPTER
THREE

Despite W.R.'s protestations and some most unladylike cussing, Stringer left the hotel a little before noon, walking sort of funny at first. The sky above was blue and clear where it wasn't smudged with smoke from the gas flares all around. The skyline in every direction was dominated by oil derricks. They looked even bigger and uglier by daylight. But nobody seemed to mind them. Almost everyone who owned an acre of land seemed to have an oil derrick on their property and those who didn't had oil lease offers posted out front. Everyone Stringer passed seemed to be in a good mood. They ranged in dress and complexion from grimy white derrick hands to cigar-store Indian, with most somewhere in between. For, just or unjust, the recent experiment of the Indian Nation had served to turn most of the population into plain old country folk of various shades. Stringer, of course, knew the Cherokee in particular had

27

been as white as Indian at the time they'd been driven
west at gunpoint. Their chief and spokesman, John
Ross, had been seven-eighths white, mostly Scottish,
and, like other prosperous Cherokee, he'd lost a fine
plantation house along with his orchards and fields of
cash crops when his white neighbors had decided he
was a dangerous savage fixing to scalp them, dressed in
his suit and tie.

The same thinking had placed the Creek Nation out
here with their traditional Cherokee enemies, with results anyone but a Washington political hack should
have foreseen. The Creek and Cherokee had delighted
in slaughtering one another long before the coming of
the white man. The Cherokee had adapted first to living
as white farmers and planters. So they'd included the
practice of keeping slaves, buying them on the same
market as their white business rivals. The Creeks, while
just as willing to try civilization, once it had whipped
them, had not only been willing to *help* escaping slaves,
but had tended to intermarry with them. Just how much
or how often was a matter of some dispute, with the
Cherokee tending to dismiss their old enemies as more
an African than American Indian nation, with the proud
and mostly pure-blooded Osage joining the Cherokee on
this point, leading to many an interesting Saturday night
just a few years back. The one good thing Stringer
could see about the oil boom was that all the local Indians might mellow some as they all got rich together.

He was pondering what that lawyer had said about
signing oil leases with Indians when he came to the
Arkansas River, running muddy under swirling oil
slicks, and had to stop. There seemed to be just as many
oil derricks and oil-spattered houses on the far side. But
there was no bridge at the end of this particular oily

street, so he turned back from the dead end. Retracing his steps, he spied an older gent sunning himself on the edge of a roadside drilling platform and since the gent seemed calm and reasonable, asked directions to the local office of the Bureau Of Indian Affairs. The old timer gave him directions, explaining the BIA was around the corner from the Western Union office near the depot. Stringer thanked him and asked, "As long as you seem up to guiding greenhorns, could you tell me why you need such towers in the sky to sink wells the other way entire?"

The old-timer spat and said, "It's too hot and dry for long lecturings. So, suffice it to say that whether you drills with an up-and-down chisel-bit or one of them newfangled rotary bits, you still got a heap of iron to lift in and outten the bore. Both ways calls for even longer lengths of pipe to line the results. They come the length of railroad flat cars, and that's a mighty tall pipe when you stands her on end. So all the lifting and dropping has to be done with block and tackle from on high until sooner or later you winds up with an oil well or a dry hole and gets to quit, see?"

Stringer glanced up at the idle cables just dangling free at the moment and said, "I can see you finished doing one or the other here." To which the old man replied with a nod, "Hit oil without as much gas as we might have liked. That's how come I get to sit here, keeping an eye on the pump 'til she settles in."

Stringer nodded at the leather belting running from a nearby tin shed to the glorified water pump in the center of the messy platform as he said, "I see what you're up to, sort of. But how come you still need that big derrick, now that it's done its job?"

The old oil man looked sincerely puzzled as he replied, "Hell, we don't need it for nothing. Why do you ask?"

Stringer said, "I was just wondering. Wouldn't it be neater to haul all that greasy timber out of the sky, once there's no call for it being there?"

The expert on the subject frowned and said, "It ain't hurting nobody. It would cost as much or more to tear it down as it did to put it it up. So why bother?"

"Wouldn't it be cheaper to use the timbers from one derrick to build another?" Stringer asked.

The old-timer shook his head and said, "I can see you ain't an oil field man. It's best to start each time with fresh timber and cut or bolt her as you build. It's mostly cheap fir or pine. So we don't build 'em to last and, like I said, nobody wants to work with the stuff once it's been throwed together and gummed up with rock-oil."

Stringer cast a sober glance at the forest of similar derricks all around as he said, "In other words, half the derricks I see right now are just standing there, waiting to fall over sooner or later?"

The older man shrugged and said, "To tell you the truth, I've never given that much thought. This field will likely be played out long before the wood rots off at the roots. So none of us will be here to worry about it, right?"

Stringer knew better than to ask whether anyone cared about the local breeds and full bloods on the day of reckoning. He just thanked the old-timer again and went on his way, perhaps a mite wiser about the oil business, but still in the dark about that shoot-out at the depot with a man said to rent his gun by the hour. For it could hardly be a closely guarded secret that this boom was a gut-and-git operation, or that the big eastern oil

trust was out to gobble up all the little boys. Teddy
Roosevelt kept saying so, every other speech, and old
John D. Rockefeller didn't seem all that worried about
it. It was no secret that old John D. was out to take over
the new industry entire. *He* made speeches, too, and
seemed to think he was doing the country a favor by
standardizing the product and fixing a set price on the
same to save folk the time and trouble of shopping
about. But while old John D. was a hard-nosed, ruthless
rascal, Stringer couldn't see him stooping to the likes of
the late Jack Holt. Standard Oil had been accused of a
lot of mean things, but murdering a man before you
tried to buy him out just wasn't their style, even if he
had something or knew something they were at all concerned about.

The local wildcatters were, of course, less predict-
able. Most of them were tinhorn operators and none had
the financial and political clout of the big boys back
East. They figured to be out to buy up such oil leases as
they could, prove a test well or more, and sell out to the
eastern trust. That did allow some slack to their business
ethics, and a tightly budgeted businessman might well
find it cheaper to hire a gun than to pay off the Fourth
Estate, assuming they were out to hide something big
enough to be worth real money.

But that was where Stringer got stuck. For as he'd
told dear little Bubbles, he'd never heard of a way to
salt an oil well, and nobody was going to talk old John
D. into buying out a dry oil lease at any price. The
stinkard who'd sent Jack Holt after him had to be afraid
he'd expose something *else*.

Stringer's train of thought was derailed by a considerable noise coming his way down the narrow, rutted
street. He glanced up to see four little Indians in a big

white Stanley Steamer bearing down on him. The
steam-driven horseless carriage made hardly any noise
at all. The four kids were screaming their heads off, as
the one at the wheel overcontrolled the speeding contraption from side to side, tearing pickets off fencing
and almost running Stringer down as he, in turn, leaped
from side to side while the big machine bore down on
him, no matter which way he jumped. In the dust cloud
behind the sidewinding Stanley, an adult male voice was
calling it all sorts of names and adding, "Somebody stop
that runaway, Goddamn it!"

Stringer knew how to stop a runaway team. He'd
never tried to stop a runaway horseless carriage before.
But he knew that unless *somebody* stopped it, the
steamer was going to deposit itself and all those kids in
the river at the dead end to the south, so he whipped out
his six-gun and shot it in the hood as it whipped by.

That worked, after a fashion. The runaway Stanley
kept going, wailing like a bansheee and spouting a sideways plume of steam that would have done Moby Dick
proud. But when Stringer chased after it, enveloped in
oil-scented hot mist, he saw it was starting to slow
down as the pressure dropped. It still had enough mass
to coast on down to the timber guard rail at the dead end
of the street, but it wasn't going fast enough to crash on
through. So when Stringer caught up with them, the
kids were picking themselves off the floor boards,
somewhat subdued.

The little Indian who'd been driving, or trying to,
was a girl of about nine in a starched white pinafore that
had likely been a lot cleaner when she'd put it on that
morning. Two of the boys were dressed like Little Lord
Fauntleroy, and the third had a dirtier face and wore
raggedy bib overalls with no shirt under it. Stringer

asked them if they were all right. The only one who answered was the little gal. She said, "*Now* you're gonna get it. Here comes Uncle Walter!"

Stringer turned the way she was looking, as a tall hatchet-faced Indian dressed like Buffalo Bill in white Stetson and matching fringed deerskin shirt bore down on them, panting for breath between curses. The Indian was wearing a brace of silver-mounted Colts as well, so Stringer didn't see any need to put his own drawn gun away until the other armed man smiled boyishly at him and said, "Wa! That was quick thinking. I never thought of *shooting* the son of a bitch when it lit out with my sister's kids like that."

Then he noticed the one raggedy little kid and added, "All but this colored boy, I mean. Mary Jane, haven't you been told not to play with colored children when I let you and your brothers drive into town with me?"

The raggedy boy scowled from the back seat and protested, "I ain't colored. I'm Creek, damn it, and it wasn't me as opened the steam throttle just to see what might happen!"

The big Indian turned back to Stringer as if for help as he explained, "Mary Jane has always been curious about mechanical contraptions. You should see what she done to her poor mother's Singer machine, trying to sew sheet tin to leather. I answer to Walter Bluefeather and I brand my cows Rocking Tipi. What do I owe you for saving these kids a drowning, Pard?"

Stringer put his gun away with a smile as he answered, "It was my pleasure, Walt, as long as you're not sore at me for blowing holes through your hood and boiler. They call me Stringer MacKail and I fear I don't know much about repairing a Stanley Steamer."

Bluefeather shrugged and said, "Hell, let her just rust

in peace. I never should have let 'em sell me such a contrary hunk of junk in the first place. Takes a quarter hour to get up the steam to go anywheres aboard her and, as you just saw, once you get a Stanley *going* they're sort of hard to *stop*. I left the kids in her with the burner going, just long enough to step into the tobacco shop for a chaw, and next thing I knew they'd took off on me like a shot."

One of the well dressed boys in the back said, "It was Mary Jane who fooled with the throttle, Uncle Walter." To which the girl replied by sticking out her tongue at him. Stringer sort of expected Walter Bluefeather to at least fuss at her, but the over-dressed Indian just said, "Let's not cry over spilt milk, kids. What say we all go back over to main street and Uncle Walter will buy you all some ice cream?" He hesitated, then told the Creek kid, "You, too, nigger boy."

The young Creek swore in his own lingo and rolled out the far side to walk off, scuffing dust and holding his head high. The dapper Bluefeather called out, "Come back here, damn it! When I offers ice cream to a kid I expects him to damn well eat it!"

But the boy he'd insulted just kept walking. Bluefeather shrugged and said, "To hell with him, then. *You* want some ice cream, don't you, MacKail?"

Stringer shook his head and said, "Not just now, thanks all the same. What do you mean to do about this steamer, here?"

Bluefeather said, "Nothing. I mean to buy me a better make in town afore we drive on home to my spread. I can afford all the autee-mobwheels I want, seeing I got a thousand head of longhorns and a dozen oil wells growing on my Rocking Tipi, now. I think I'd best spring for a Panard or a Buick, this time. I doubt Mary

Jane, here, could crank a gas engine, willful as she may be."

As the five of them headed back to the center of town, Stringer allowed Mary Jane would likely bust a gut, or her arm, trying to start an internal combustion banger. But he couldn't help observing, "Oil leases must pay well indeed if you can afford to be so casual about your property, Walt."

As the children skipped ahead, Bluefeather explained, "At a nickel a barrel, all day and all night, the money do roll in. To tell the truth, a nickel a barrel didn't strike me as all that much, when they first offered it. But when you consider how fast and how steady them oil wells piss the stuff, them nickles add up faster than we can spend 'em."

The tall Indian spat and added, "It ain't as if we haven't been *trying*, you understand."

Stringer nodded and said, "I noticed you dressed both yourself and the kids sort of prosperous. But tell me something. What happens once the oil runs dry?"

Bluefeather spat again and replied, "I'll be in a fix the day my *heart* stops pumping, too. In the meanwhile, why worry about things that ain't fixing to take place all that soon? They tell me this Tulsa field ought to last to the end of this century at the rate the country's burning rock-oil. I'd sure like to be around that long. But, to tell the truth, I ain't betting on it."

Stringer grimaced and said, "Well, it's your oil and your future. You could even be right, if they keep making engines and oil furnaces at the current rate. No offense, Walt, but if I had an oil well I'd bank some of the money and be sort of careful about the way I spent the rest."

Bluefeather chuckled and said, "I thought MacKail

was a Scotch name. None of you palefaces really know how to enjoy life. I'll tell you what I'll do. I'll meet you here a hundred years from now and we'll compare notes on which of us had the most fun."

Stringer didn't answer. He'd been chided about his own easy way with money from time to time. Blue-feather did seem to be overdoing it a mite. But it was none of his beeswax if the suddenly rich cuss wound up old and broke.

Stringer could see how, in a way, the oil well Indians of Oklahoma Territory could be enjoying a delicious joke on the white man. For the white man had pushed them onto this dry and mostly worthless range against their will and now, instead of dying off as old Andrew Jackson had no doubt figured they might, they were getting rich, hand over fist, without any effort on their part. It sort of made a man believe there might be a Just God, after all.

He parted friendly with the big and little Indians in front of the nearest ice cream parlor, then he strode on to Main Street and First, near the railroad depot. Finding the new office of the BIA was easy enough. When he went inside it looked like the hiring hall for Buffalo or Pawnee Bill's Wild West Show. Both Bills hired lots of cowboys and Indians.

Everyone seemed to be dressed similarly as they shared hardwood benches to either side of the reception desk. The Gibson Girl behind the desk asked him what tribe he claimed membership in and looked sort of relieved when the tall, tanned and blond Stringer showed her his press pass, handed her a business card, and said he wasn't there to ask for any money. She told him to have a seat and carried his card back into the maze of cubby hole offices.

Stringer hunkered in a corner and had a Bull Durham just about built when she came back and waved him over to confide that the agency manager would be proud to give him an interview. He got lost a couple of times among the open-desk offices that slightly resembled whorehouse cribs, save that everyone in them was sitting up with all their duds on. When at last he found a real door with the right name on it and went in, a portly white man wearing a tweed suit and a harrassed expression waved him to a seat near the desk and began by saying, "It's about time someone from the newspapers asked to hear our side instead of just printing more lies about us screwing Mister Lo, the poor Indian. I'm surprised you're not here to apply for a Cherokee allotment. Half the so-called Cherokee are as white as you or me, you know."

Stringer held up his freshly rolled smoke for permission, got a nod, and lit it before he said, "That's one of the things I'd like to get straight in my head, Mister, ah, Manson. Might you be one of the Scotch Mansons of Clan Gunn, by the way?"

The portly Indian agent shrugged and said, "I know my folk were Scotch, a long time back. Can't stay if they belonged to any clan or not. Why do you ask?"

Stringer said, "I've noticed some of *us* are sort of vague on past tribes we might have belonged to a ways back. Just how might the BIA define membership in one tribe of Indians or another, seeing as so many Oklahoma folk look white or colored to me?"

Manson sighed and asked, "You noticed? These days we've got Wannabees of every shade from Lily White to Inky Black collecting handouts from Washington."

Stringer raised an eyebrow to ask, "Wannabee?" to which the agent answered with a bitter laugh, "I wanna

be an Indian. Just a few years back we couldn't keep a
full blood on the reservation and most breeds would
cuss you if you hinted they might have just a drop or
more of Indian blood. Now every trash white or colored
cow hand west of the big Muddy suddenly seems to
recall an Indian great grandmother the family had forgotten all about."

Manson got out a cigar of his own, and bit off and
spat the end on the floor as he explained, "In it's infinite
wisdom, the U.S. Government never got around to de-
fining just how much Indian blood one needed to be
called an Indian, as long as you didn't want to scalp
anyone. The Five Civilized Tribes bitched, with some
justification, that they were part white before we moved
them out there in the first place. Old Hickory allowed it
didn't matter and that an Indian was any person who
belonged to any Indian tribe, or nation, as they prefer to
call it."

He waved at the shelves of buckram-bound law
books just to Stringer's right as he added, "Indian Policy, if you want to call it that, has been changed over the
years with each new administration. President Roosevelt's dream is to have them all educated and assimi-
lated by the middle of this century. God knows what the
Democrats will do, once *they're* back in. As of now,
don't hold me to it, the old Indian Nation has been more
or less transformed into the new Territory of Oklahoma
and I sure hope you don't intend to print that as an
attempt to screw the Indian."

As the red-faced Manson lit his cigar, Stringer asked
just what the change was supposed to do for Mister Lo,
adding, "I thought the Indians enjoyed having their own
nation, once they got used to life out here."

Manson blew smoke out his nostrils like a fly-blown

bull and said, "It never worked worth a damn. Each tribe applied for and got its own patch of what we now call Oklahoma. The so-called Indian Nation never took up half of what we hope to make a future state. Each tribe was granted its own government, under tribal councils supervised by Washington. That's why we've always had so many federal marshals here to deal with the sad results, to the best of their ability, see?"

Stringer shook his head and said, "Not really." So Manson explained, "Let me give you an easy example. Do you remember the infamous Belle Starr?"

Stringer said, "Not personally. I've seen two tintypes of the lady. Both were ugly and they struck me as two different ladies entire."

Manson nodded and said, "Fort Smith photographers have no shame when asked for pictures of dead folk by you newspaper gents. Never mind what she looked like. What she was doing down the river at Younger's Bend was selling moonshine and dealing in stolen goods. Her spread lay in the Cherokee Strip or tribal reserve. She had no lawful right to be there, seeing she was pure white as well as just awful, until it occurred to her to marry up with an otherwise worthless Cherokee named Sam Starr. That made her Cherokee, as far as the tribal council cared. The white lightning she sold no doubt confused them on the finer points of anthropology and, with the Cherokee claiming her as one of their own, the federal government couldn't do a thing about her squatting on reservation land. But as a white woman, any time she was off the Cherokee Strip, she was free to do business as a white, and did. She got a pretty penny for the livestock Starr and his gang stole."

Stringer repressed a yawn and started to say something dumb about ancient history, the lady in question having been shot in the back just before the turn of the century. Then he brightened and said, "Hold on. Are you saying an Indian still can't sign a bill of sale like anyone else?"

Manson nodded and said, "Not if he's on the BIA rolls as a reservation Indian. Under federal statute law, all Indians in theory, and all reservation Indians in practice, are wards of the government, the same as minors or certified half-wits. It was intended for their own protection, lest some white slicker 'em with gold bricks. No contract an Indian signs with a white man has any validity in court. Didn't you know that?"

Stringer said, "I do now, and you say you have all sorts of folk *asking* you to let 'em be Indians?"

Manson nodded and sighed, "It beats working. We keep trying to settle Indian claims with a final cash payment. They usually take the money. But then they usually seem to find a lawyer to take us around the same old mullberry bush. Back in the nineties, when it became obvious the Indians were only using part of this territory and that white outlaws and squatters seemed hell-bent on using the rest, the government gave cash and land deeds to each and every Indian family so the sooners could come in and lay claim to the rest. It worked just swell until the money was spent, they noticed they weren't going to get any more handouts, and screamed they hadn't read the fine print. That's what I'm doing out here now, trying to tidy up the mess. You'd be surprised how many long-lost relatives turn up to demand their own share of the tribal lands, once you discover oil under it."

Stringer smiled thinly and said, "No, I wouldn't. It's just as well I never had a Cherokee great grandmother. I've always wanted to get rich quick and easy. So how do you decide whether one of your Wannabees is the real thing, and what does he get from you if you can't prove he's Swedish?"

Manson shrugged and said, "It's up to the tribal councils to decide who they let in and who they don't. Our hands are tied. Our only hope is that, now that tribal lands are *worth* something, the tribal leaders may be more picky than they were in old Belle Starr's day."

Stringer nodded and said, "I'd hesitate to share my slice of the pie with a long-lost cousin I never heard of before. But I'm still confused about the way a real or Wannabee Indian deals in oil leases if no contract between a white and Indian cuts any legal ice."

Manson said, "You get a white sponsor to sign for you, naturally. Those gents waiting out front who don't want to be Indians likely want to be given power of attorney for one, see?"

Stringer raised an eyebrow to ask, "Is such power an easy thing to come by?" To which Manson answered with a scowl, "I pride myself on making it as tough as I can. But we can't do much about a white approved of by the tribal council as a spouse or legal guardian. The B.I.A. has no jurisdiction over business contracts signed by whites, while the tribal councils say it's none of our business if some mighty tolerant white person wants to marry or adopt an Indian. I just *told* you Indian Policy was a confusing mess."

Stringer said, "Well, money does draw lawyers the way shit draws flies, and lawyers are paid to look for loopholes. I just met an oil well Indian called Walter Bluefeather. He surely made an oil deal with somebody. I don't suppose you know of him?"

Manson suppressed a moan and said, "I wish I didn't. He's a member of the Osage tribal council and a real pain in the ass. He had more land than we ever allotted him before they struck oil under it. He's a shrewd businessman who'd bought out other Osage to expand his cattle spread before the first test well was sunk. He hasn't gotten any poorer since. I think he signed with Standard Oil."

Stringer insisted, "How? You just told me he couldn't do that, didn't you?"

Manson nodded and said, "He's married to a white woman. She, in turn, is related to a white lawyer. Need I say more?"

Stringer replied, "I wish you would. I don't see why Uncle Sam makes it so *complicated* for folk to do what they're going to do in any case. It seems to me that even a dumb Indian is as likely to be cheated by a white signing an oil lease for him as he is by the better-known gents out to buy his oil."

Manson shrugged and said, "I don't write the regulations. You don't have to worry about Walter Blue-feather, though. He's smarter and tougher than he looks and he has the Osage tribal government behind him. But I could tell you tales about less bright-eyed and bushy-tailed redskins."

Stringer glanced at the wall clock. Then he nodded half to himself and said, "Just tell me one." So the Indian agent told him, "You're right. I do have to get back to work. To make it short and sour, I know of one old Creek with a drinking problem who was pleasantly surprised to discover a red-headed fancy gal from Fort Smith was suddenly in love with him. But she held out for a ring and got it, less than a week before Sinclair Oil got to him with an offer that needed the signature of a voting citizen of These United States."

Stringer asked, "Are gals allowed to vote in Oklahoma?" To which Manson replied, prim-lipped, "No more than Indians of either sex. But the new bride had a trusted white male friend, as some call pimps in Fort Smith. The old Creek let his wife and her real lover make the deal for him. Since the contract was signed by his white sponsor, guess who got the front-money check, and cashed it without bothering the old Creek about it? I suppose they felt as long as they kept him well likkered up at their own modest expense he had nothing to complain about. He didn't complain, as a matter of fact, until the drillers sinking the test well on his property wound up with a dry hole. Then they went away, his wife and her pimp went away, and he was left with an awesome hang-over and a big mess in his front yard. I told him, when he came bitching to us, that he should have showed up sooner."

Stringer snuffed out the last of his smoke and got to his feet as he asked, "Could you have done anything for the lovestruck Indian if he had?" and Manson said, "Sure we could have. Unless an Indian client of the BIA chooses his or her own white sponsor the BIA stands ready to supply an agency lawyer to do things right. It takes more time, of course, and for some reason some Indians don't seem to think we have their best interests at heart. But I want you to print it in your paper that to date no Indian who's made an oil deal with BIA approval and backing has been screwed out of one wooden nickel!"

They shook on that and Stringer left to dig for more leads.

CHAPTER
FOUR

Stringer headed for a nearby saloon as the next best thing to a barber shop if one wanted to listen to small town gossip.

The joint was a hole in the wall no more than twenty feet wide with the bar running along one wall back to darker smoke-filled depths where an invisible player piano was playing a mechanical ragtime tune. Stringer would have had a time admiring the wonderous invention had there been more light and less smoke. For, despite the hour of the afternoon, the dinky drinking establishment was sardine-packed with gents who smelled like rock-oil or cowshit, depending on how they were dressed. Most of the crowd seemed to be oil field hands. A few dressed more like shop clerks were likely oil field deal makers, judging from the way they talked. One or two cow hands along the length of the bar could have been breeds or even full bloods. It was against the law to serve Indians hard liquor, but the fat gal behind the bar was paid to peddle booze, not to act as a deputy marshal or even a reservation police officer, so she didn't even study Stringer's face for signs of Indian ancestry when he asked for a boiler maker. She just made him pay before she served him.

The beer chaser was good. The shot glass of red-eye she served with it tasted like paint remover. He was a good sport about it. He knew it was his own fault for ordering hard liquor in moonshine country and decided to just stick to beer from then on.

As a well-traveled westerner, Stringer knew the secret of avoiding fights until one had been accepted in a neighborhood saloon was to just drink quietly and not stare at any of the regulars until spoken to. But when the building and the ground under it shook and the roar of not too distant thunder rattled the one glass window to his left, Stringer found himself blurting, "Jesus, what was that?" to nobody in particular.

The man to his right dressed like an oil rigger chuckled and said, "Nitro. Sounds like Tiger Twain is at it again. Old Tiger has always used more nitro than patience with a stubborn formation. One of these days he's going to overdo it. But what the hell, I've told him to his face I'll never work with him again."

Stringer finished his first beer, signaled the barmaid to serve them both again, and said, "I think I met old Tiger last night. Just after he'd lubricated this hat for me. I can't say I recall him chucking nitroglycerine down the pipe, though."

The oil rigger nodded and explained, "He's got a dozen rigs drilling for old Blackjack Sinclair. I heard about the gusher they brung in last night. I'd say that blast come from a deeper drill farther west and higher up. They found those fool blackjack oaks growing in an old graveyard atop a rise and so down they went. I hear she's down more than a mile and still dry as the Indian bones they hit six feet down."

A man in a business suit on the far side of the oil rigger chimed in, "Blackjack Sinclair is buggy as a hobo's bedroll. There's nothing scientific about his crazy hunches."

The oil rigger nodded but said, "I can't see why I'd want to grow over an oil dome if I was an oak tree, neither. But you got to admit old Sinclair's struck a hell of a lot of oil in his short time as a wildcatter." Then he turned to Stringer and held out a hand grimed with ground-in dirt, saying, "When a man offers me a beer I like to know his name. I'd be Bull Durham if it's all the same with you."

Stringer shook with him as he said with a smile, "I've been smoking your cigarettes for years, Mister Durham."

The oil rigger grimaced and said, "That sure was original on your part. My folk Christened me Leroy, back in Penn State. But others made the connection betwixt Bull and Durham shortly thereafter."

Stringer said, "I started out Stuart instead of Stringer MacKail. I suspect I come out ahead, but folk will shorten Stuart to Stu, if you let 'em, and I even hate stew on a plate."

They clinked glasses on it while, oblivious to the ritual from where he was drinking on the far side, the more formally dressed oil expert proclaimed, "There's no mystery about the way Sinclair strikes oil. He hears of an oil strike made by gents who know what they're about and muscles in. You could sink a well most anywhere in this county with a fair chance of striking rock-oil. We're over an underground sea of the stuff. It's all one formation, right?"

Bull Durham smiled knowingly at Stringer and said, "Gee, I wish I knew so much about geology. I'd get to wear a white shirt every day and all the gals would love me."

Stringer smiled back less certainly and asked, "Well, *isn't* this Tulsa field more or less one formation, once you get down to it?"

Bull Durham replied, "Yes and no. Oil floats on water, with a lot of gas mixed in with it. The oil and gas in these parts would have fizzed up out of the earth years ago if it wasn't for a thick layer of cap-rock holding 'em down like the lid on a pressure cooker. Picture that cap-rock more like a wrinkled blanket than a dead-flat lid and you'll see why there's more to a producing well than sticking a needle in a rubber balloon."

Durham swallowed some beer before adding, "Like I said, the stuff you want floats on water. Hot salty water, left over from some ocean they must have had around here one time. You got to drill where the cap-rock blisters higher, full of gas and rock-oil. Drill where the blanket dips down the *other* way and all you drill into is wet sand, which we still call a dry hole. I don't know why that graveyard they just drilled down through don't seem to be above a rise instead of a dip. It sound like it ought to be, oak trees betwixt the tombstones or no. But as I discovered the one time I worked with Tiger Twain, he just hates to drill one inch deeper than he has to. So let's hope that blast we just felt did her for him. He'd likely to bust every window in town before he'll admit it's a dry hole."

Stringer asked just what pouring nitroglycerine down the pipe had to do with finding rock oil. Bull Durham said, "Hell, you don't *pour* nitro down a well. You want it to go off at the *bottom*. You puts it in a can or bottle with a dynamite cap and a mighty long electric fuse. The resulting explosion a mile or so down would sound a mite louder if anyone was down there to listen."

Stringer nodded and said, "I did feel that last blast with my feet more than I heard it with my ears. But what's all that underground noise supposed to do for the oil industry?"

Bull Durham explained patiently, "Bust the shit out of the formation, of course. Sometimes there's enough oil in the rock to pay, but not enough gas to shove it into the hole. You got to understand that oil don't sit underground in buried frog ponds. It's there betwixt sand grains or even in the pores of harder rock. Cracking the rock all apart lets the oil seep outten the cracks and into the well, if there's any oil there at all. You might say nitro is the last resort, unless you're talking about Tiger Twain. He takes too many chances for *this* child to work with!"

As if to prove his point, they were treated to another foot tingle just before the window glass rattled in time with the dulcet tones of another blast. The bar maid swore and Durham growled, "He's gone just plain crazy this afternoon. There's no way they could have test pumped since that last fool blast."

Stringer found the conversation interesting. But then he heard a more ominous rumble from deeper in the depths of the tough little joint and cocked an ear to hear some invisible tough complaining, "Jesus, do you have to keep feeding nickles into that fool piano? I can't stand that nigger music they got on the damned old roll."

Stringer couldn't hear the softer reply to the complaint about ragtime music. But he could guess the gist of it when the same complaining voice complained louder, "God damn it, I mean it! I'm from Texas myself, and if you start that uppity nigger music up again you're surely going to hear Dixie, played on your Damnyankee skull!"

Stringer finished the last of his schooner and left before

the fight started. He asked directions out front and headed for the scene of action the *San Francisco Sun* was more apt to find worth printing. It was getting hotter as the day wore on and the old Indian graveyard turned out a longer walk than he enjoyed in high heeled Justins.

But he kept going when he heard another muffled explosion just as he was considering turning back. So, in time, he came to the outskirts of the little town, although the forest of oil derricks extended well out across the rolling range to the west, and since a lot of folk seemed to be standing around a raw timber derrick atop a hill near the winding Arkansas to his left, he just ambled on up it.

Having shortcut across the slope of summer-kilt grass, he had to climb through the barbed wire fence around the old graveyard once he got to it. He was glad it was broad daylight, for the acre or more of grave markers, partly shaded by young but brooding blackjack oaks, was depressing enough as it was. Most of the graves were marked by sun-silvered wooden crosses with a slate of sandstone slab rising here and there. Some of the graves had little picket fences around them. One fence had been freshly whitewashed and there were wilted flowers on the grave of a little girl named Alice who'd have been almost grown today, had she lived. But most of the graves didn't look as if they'd been visited in recent memory and the weeds between them grew almost knee deep. Stringer strode on to the drilling platform spread across at least four graves under the looming oil rig just in time to wonder if he hadn't avoided one drunken brawl just to wander into another.

For if Tiger Twain wasn't drunk, he was making noise enough for three such gents as he cussed at that same lawyer he'd been talking to the night before, a lot more quietly.

Stringer had to circle the platform and drift closer before he could hear what Lawyer Lacey had to say about whatever might be going on. When Stringer could make out his softer but just as stubborn words, he decided the lawyer was making the most sense. Lacey didn't want Tiger to drop any more bombs down the pipe. He said, "You'd have never drilled this site in the first place if I hadn't been overruled by those damned oak trees. We don't have full clearance on some of these graves and we're likely to be sued over the damage you've done up here already. I told you the Creek tribal council gave us permission to drill between the gate and the first row of markers but, all right, what's done is done and just don't damage any others."

Tiger replied as his four man crew and the curious crowd of others who'd beaten Stringer to the scene tried not to look as if they were taking sides, "Shit, I never drilled through no old Creek who could have noticed. We moved the damned markers with tender loving care afore we put up the rig. They're piled neat as hell, over there by yonder gate."

Lawyer Lacey sniffed and pointed the other way with his chin as he replied, "That blasting has made leaning towers out of a good dozen more and I say we should quit while we're ahead."

Tiger sneered, "It's a good thing you ain't in charge of this crew, then. I got me some cap-rock to punch through and the bit just won't do it without some help."

Lacey protested, "Damn it, Tiger, I know you consider me a desk-bound pencil pusher. But I did start out in the Penn State fields and a man does learn a lot about oil wells settling damage claims in court. You're not supposed to blast cap-rock open from the top. It's too dangerous. It's like lancing a boil with a ball peen hammer. Why don't you just change bits and do it the regular way, damn it?"

Tiger waved a grimy hand at a pile of what looked to be oversized crowbars to Stringer as he snapped, "I've worn out a dozen damn bits to no avail on that last yard of damn rock down yonder. It's hard as granite, even if it is supposed to be shale. I'm having enough of a time cracking it with nitro. So why don't you go back to the office and see if you can sharpen pencils neat? Us working stiffs ain't *paid* to be neat. There's an oil dome under this damned hill and I mean to punch me a *hole* through it. So get outten my way afore I punch a hole through your fool *skull*, you necktie-wearing pain in the ass!"

Lacey blanched and took a step backward. Then he sniffed and said, "We'd best see what Mister Sinclair has to say about all this. Meanwhile, I'm ordering you not to use any more nitro up here and that's my last word on the subject for now."

Tiger laughed and said, "All right. I heard you. Now get the hell outten my hair." Then he turned around to tell one of his roughnecks, "Get the next can of nitro, Slim. Charlie, you test the battery box. I'll fuse her to the wire once we know we have the juice to work with."

Lawyer Lacey swore softly and dropped off the platform. As he headed for the graveyard gate to the west, Stringer was torn between curiosities. Watching them set another charge and detonate it promised to be interesting. On the other hand, Lawyer Lacey seemed to be headed for a one horse surrey parked under the trees by the side of the only road off this hill and it was a good walk back to town. Stringer decided he already knew as much about blasting a stubborn oil well as Sam Barca would want to run in the *Sun*, while the lawyer had just raised another question about Indian rights. So he tagged along after the upset lawyer and caught up just as Lacey was untethering his draft horse. Stringer introduced himself and said, "I know you don't remember me. But I was at that other well in the center of town last night."

Lacey nodded and said, "I remember you. I thought you were just a nosy cowboy who liked to listen to the grown-ups talk. I'm not sure I like you better as a news-paper man. The oil business is a sort of secretive game, played for high stakes, and my company hands out press releases whenever it has anything it wants its rivals to read in the papers."

Stringer tried, "That's likely why John D. and the other oil barons make Teddy Roosevelt so mad. The trouble with keeping secret all the moves you make from the general public is that said public just has to *guess*, and you know how folk gossip about things they know little or nothing about. Have you heard about that inventor who comes up with a way to make horseless carriages run hundreds of miles on one gallon, and how Standard Oil bought him out and destroyed his plans lest poor honest motorists get a fair shake at the gas pumps?"

Lacey groaned and said, "I thought we just murdered widows and orphans to render down as motor oil. I'll give you a ride back to town. I'll even tell you what I think of Standard Oil. But don't ask me any questions about my *own* outfit."

Stringer agreed and they got in the surrey. Lacey clucked his horse on up the slope to where the weedy road was wide enough to swing around the right way. Then the nag in front of them shied and took the bit in her teeth to bolt, as the earth quivered under her hooves and the roar over by the oil rig in the graveyard seemed to keep getting louder and louder instead of fading away.

Lawyer Lacey hauled back on the reins as hard as he was able. But he wasn't able to stop a spooked nag with other things on her dull mind. She just wanted to put some distance between them and that awful roaring to her east. So she bolted west, along the crest of the ridge and to hell with any road.

Stringer stood up, braced one boot on the dashboard, and dove over it to land face down on the back of the spooked runaway. He grabbed the brass knobs of her horse collar and hauled himself into a sitting position with one boot braced on either wooden shaft as he hauled back on the reins with little more luck than the lawyer hauling the same from behind him. Then Stringer stretched forward enough to grab the cheek-strap of the bridle and crank the nag's neck back to one side. That and running into a clump of Osage orange brush slowed her down enough for Stringer to roll off, brace both boot heels, and stop her entire with a palm cupped over her muzzle. She was still upset as hell, but he was able to control her now, soothing, "Take it easy, if you ever want to breathe again. Haven't you ever heard a bitty explosion before, old girl?"

Then he glanced back the way they'd just come to add, "Oh, Jesus H. Christ!" as the shaken Lawyer Lacey wailed, "I knew it! Look what that fool's gone and done!"

Stringer was looking. The top of the oil derrick had been blown to oil-soaked kindling and replaced by a twenty story column of greenish black oil and gas. Stringer forgave the spooked nag he was hanging on to when he saw the wind was from the west. For what goes up must come down and the stinky black rain of rock-oil was coming down on all those old graves in a way they'd never meant to be watered. Even as they watched, a river of the stuff had formed to run down into the nearby Arkansas, which was supposed to be a river of water to the folk down stream who used it.

Lawyer Lacey shouted, "Get that bit back in place and let's get back to town! I have wires to get off to the home office and it still won't be soon enough!"

Stringer slipped the bit back behind the nag's teeth and ran to join Lacey in the surrey as it commenced to roll. He had a wire or two to send, now that there seemed to be a real story. As they got under way he grunted, "I see what you meant about lancing a boil with a ball peen hammer. How do you go about capping a gusher when it's coming up through a busted open formation instead of a pipe?"

Lacey almost sobbed, "You don't. That son of a bitching Tiger has let it all loose at once. So we're in about as bad a mess as I feared we might be!"

Then they both discovered he was wrong when they were almost blown off the seat by a gust of oven-hot wind and the runaway gusher was replaced by a towering mushroom cloud of smoke and flame. Lacey wailed, "Oh, shit, it's caught fire!" to which Stringer could only reply, "I noticed.' as he braced himself to leap off and head back to the disaster site. He knew Lacey wasn't about to stop. Then, as they tore down the slope, he saw other rigs coming up it, while distant bells rang all over town and so, seeing as much help as *he* could hope to offer was on the way, he decided he'd best beat sweet little Bubbles to the Western Union office with the scoop.

He didn't. As they leaped down from the surrey in front of the telegraph office, he saw a familiar figure in line well ahead of them. It was hard to say why all the others wanted to send wires at the same time, but they seemed intent on doing so as soon as possible, and when Lawyer Lacey tried to shove into the line, yelling that he had important business to wire his home office, he got shoved on his ass and told in no uncertain terms where the end of the line was.

Stringer doubted W.R. Hackman would punch a fellow member of the Fourth Estate, but the gents behind her might if she let anyone in ahead of her. As if she'd felt his eyes on the back of her head, T.R. turned demurely, spotted Stringer way behind her, and favored him with a sweet smile and a helpless shrug. Stringer muttered, "Yep, that's life, and I'm sure Sam Barca will understand my letting her scoop us if I explain how great she is betwixt the sheets. There has to be a better way."

There was possibly another way, at least. Stringer knew he was sunk in any case if the *L.A. Examiner* beat them by the good hour's lead she had on him at the rate this fool line seemed to be moving. So he ran for their hotel with his fingers mentally crossed and, to his relief, saw the lobby was empty and that nobody else had thought of Alexander Graham Bell, yet.

The little breed switchboard operator behind the hotel desk was only on duty during daylight hours. But he'd noticed her board when he'd checked in the night before. He gave the desk clerk a fistful of loose change to avoid needless discussion as he rolled over the fake marble and told the gal at the hotel switchboard to ring up the *San Francisco Sun* for him as he plunked a silver dollar down beside her. She blinked and stammered, "Are we talking about a call to a newspaper in San Francisco, sir, long-distance?"

He leaned against the wall beside her stool, seeing this was going to take some tedious explaining, and said, "I never said San Francisco was a *short* distance from Tulsa, Ma'am. You know more than I do about running this switchboard. But I do know it can be done, if you set your mind to it."

She said, "Gee, I don't know. The longest distance call I've ever made was to Ohio and it was a real bother. There's no line from here to there and I had to call Kansas City and ask the supervisor there for help."

He nodded and said, "Bueno. K.C. ought to be on the main cross-country line. Call them and say it's a person to person collect call, MacKail to Barca at the *San Francisco Sun* on Montgomery Street. The Frisco operator will have their number listed but I reckon I have it written down here, somewheres, if that don't work. Am I going too fast for you?"

She pouted her kissable lower lip at him and said, "Pick up the house phone on that desk yonder. I know how to get through to Kansas City, at least, and why did you say bueno? Do I look Spanish to you?"

He reached for the french phone on the fake marble counter as he soothed, "No. *I* do. I was raised in Spanish speaking country and I'll bet you another dollar you can't work those plugs any faster."

She sniffed, did some mysterious things with her rats' nest of wires, got a wrong number by mistake and then she smiled smugly and said, "Hello, Tulsa Central? This is Irene at the Osage Inn. I want to put through a collect person to person call to San Francisco, California, by way of the Kansas City long lines. Can we do that?"

They must have been able to. For as Stringer put his own hand set to one ear he heard the perky little breed repeat her question to yet another operator, who allowed she'd try. Then there was just a lot of buzzing in his ear until a ghostly distant voice said, "San Francisco Central." So Stringer read his paper's office number off his press pass and asked if there was some way to get a better connection. The operator he was next to turned to give him a dirty look as the Frisco operator told him he wasn't supposed to talk until she had his number if you please. Stringer grinned at the pretty breed and whispered, "How was I to know you gals had a guild?"

Then, though the connection was no better, there was no way to mistake the snarl of old Sam Barca in the press room of the *Sun* as he snapped, "Feature editor and what's it to you?"

Stringer asked, "Sam?" and when Barca shot back that he was hardly the Czar Of All The Russians, Stringer explained, "I'm calling from Tulsa." Then the operator cut in on them to say, "Not yet, you're not. Do you accept the charges for this call, Mister Barca?" To which Sam replied, "Yeah, yeah, get out of my damned ear. You still there, Stringer? What's going on, and it had better be good!"

Stringer gave him a quick run down on the explosion and fire atop Missionary Ridge, as he'd heard it called when he'd asked how to get there. Then he suggested, "I'll get back to you as soon as I can with any casualty figures and just what anyone hopes to do about it. As of now, I can only tell you gas and oil are going up in mighty expensive smoke and the Arkansas River is carrying one hell of an oil slick they won't much like when it passes New Orleans. That ought to be worth a headline, at least."

Barca answered, "I'll get it right to the news desk. But what about the feature I sent you after in the first place?"

Stringer said, "I haven't written it yet. There's more local color than I've been able to sort out. Some of it took some shots at me last night. He was an otherwise unimportant hired gun named Holt. I thought at first he was trying to keep me from covering the news here. But, as you see, I was covering it pretty good when that oil dome burst open just now. I'll get back to you, Sam."

But Barca wailed, "Hold on! You say you were in a

gunfight and you don't call that news? Give me the damned details, you damned idjet!"

But Stringer said, "Aw, Sam, you know I don't do Wild West features on my fool *self*. It's tough enough to get folk to talk to me when they don't have me down as a gunslinger. I'll write Holt up if and when I find out there's more to his story than a surly disposition. I have no idea why he started up with me. What kind of a story is that?"

Barca said, "Pass that name by me again and let me work on it from this end. Are you sure he wasn't a Frisco tough who might have followed you to Tulsa?"

Stringer said, "His name was Jack Holt. The law here has him down as a Texas pest and he was already in Tulsa when I got here. Let me worry about him, for now. Like I said, he may have been just ornery by nature."

Barca agreed, grudgingly, and hung up without saying adios. As Stringer hung up at his end both the desk clerk and telephone operator were staring at him owl-eyed. He smiled, handed the gal another silver dollar, and said, "You see, it wasn't all that hard to make such a long-distance call, after all."

The breed gal called Irene said, "It was thrilling. You must be about the most thrilling guest we've had here for some time!"

The clerk nodded and said, "John Wesley Hardin stayed here one night, but that was before our time."

Stringer assured them he hardly enjoyed the rep of the late John Wesley Hardin and rolled back over the desk to give them back some room. As he headed back outside, a burly gent in a checked suit with a press pass in the band of his brown derby bulled in the other way to dash over to the desk and ask if there was any way he could make a long-distance call to El Paso.

Irene said, "I don't know. There might be. Now that

I'm sort of getting the hang of long-distance. This surely is becoming a more interesting job since folks struck oil under Tulsa."

Stringer didn't linger to listen. He knew what the rival newspaper man had to tell his own editor and, what the hell, as long as the *Sun* had scooped the whole country, he could afford to be a live-and-let-live gent about it.

CHAPTER
FIVE

By sundown Stringer had found a safer saloon to gossip in, enjoyed a decent supper, and taken down enough shorthand notes to justify another long-distance call to his boss. This time Sam Barca switched the call to the out-of-town news desk so he wouldn't have to write it down himself. Aware of the awesome bills they were running up with Alexander Bell, Stringer reported tersely that two oil rig hands and an innocent bystander had been killed, nobody else had been seriously singed, and that while Sinclair Oil no longer had anyone called Tiger Twain on its payroll it was doing its best to put out the fire and cap the runaway well. The editor at the far end asked how soon Stringer figured they'd be able to manage that and was told, "Not soon. The oil and gas isn't gushing out a regular bore-hole. Twain busted the shale like a pane of glass and the stuff is boiling up through a city lot of cracks and more serious fissures.

The crater at the top is fifty or more feet across. Nobody can get close enough to measure it exactly. An oil man I just talked to says there's just no way to put out the pillar of fire and that they'll just have to let her burn until all the gas escapes. That could take from any minute to a year or so from now. It depends on how much there was down there before they messed up and turned an oil well into a man-made volcano."

The editor agreed he'd never try to drill an oil well from the top using nitroglycerine, and they hung up. Then Stringer frowned down at the pretty breed operator and muttered, "Oh, Lord, I forgot to mention the Creek tribal council. But that's all right. I don't know who gets to sue whom about all that oil money going up in smoke, yet."

He cradled the desk phone and asked her, "I don't suppose you'd know anything about Creek oil leases, right?"

She scowled and snapped, "I'm part Comanche if you don't mind! First you call me a Mex and now you're trying to call me a durned old Creek!"

He smiled down at her soothingly and said, "I meant no harm, Miss Irene. I just need answers to some questions only a Creek might be able to answer. But lest I make any more mistakes about your family tree, ain't we sort of off the reservation if we're Comanche?"

She shrugged and said, "Nobody related to me ever lived on the BIA blanket. My dear mother was related to Chief Puma but she was living white when my dear old dad married up with her, down Texas way. As to what I'm doing here in what's left of the Indian Nation, I got tired of answering questions about my complexion ever' time I applied for a job."

He nodded understandingly and said, "I won't ask

you any more, then. You sure run that switchboard good. Did that other newspaper man get through to his own editor, earlier?"

She grinned up at him roguishly and confided, "No. I just wasn't able to complete his long-distance call for him. He never bet me any money that I could and he wasn't even a guest at this hotel."

Stringer laughed and said, "He must not have been out in the field as long as I have." To which she replied with an admiring nod, "Anyone can see you're a man who's been all over and dealt with all sorts of quality folk. It was a lot of fun talking to those other gals in bigger cities. Do you reckon a gal like me could get a job in San Francisco?"

He shrugged and said, "Well, they do have a couple of Frisco operators who talk Chinese. I can't say how blonde they may or may not be. You'd do better taking it up with the telephone company. I've never asked them for a job."

She said she meant to. She sounded like she might have just glimpsed new horizons. Stringer was glad for her. He didn't want to get her hopes up higher than they already seemed to be. So he refrained from mentioning that Indians were treated with more respect on the coast, where they were apt to run into fewer whites holding grudges from the recent past. The coast tribes had been about wiped out before they could be much of a bother to anyone. So naturally they were remembered fondly.

He asked Irene if any other hotel guests had made any recent long-distance calls. She shook her head and said no. That meant old Bubbles was either ignorant of modern communication or hadn't come home yet. There was no decent way to ask one gal if another gal was up in her room, or his, right now. So he decided to smoke out front a spell and see if Bubbles came back or, failing that, try his luck upstairs if Bubbles didn't show by darkness. He knew few unescorted she-males would be out after dark in a town like this unless it was mighty important.

He found a rocking chair on the hotel porch and sat down to build a cigarette. He'd just sealed the straw-colored paper with his tongue when he was joined on the porch by Chris Madsen, Bill Tilghman's deputy. The husky Dane said, "Finding you here saves me climbing the stairs. Bill sent me to have a word with you. I was hoping to find you here at the hotel."

Stringer repressed a grimace as he pictured the federal man banging on his door while he was banging Bubbles. He lit the smoke he'd just rolled and said, "You found me enjoying the cool shades of evening. What can I do for you, Chris?"

Madsen said, "Heard you was in the Pronghorn when that shoot-out commenced, earlier today."

Stringer frowned and replied, "I was there, drinking and jawing near the door. If there was a shoot-out, I'm glad I left when I did. I did hear a discussion of piano-roll music taking place in the back of the joint. I can't say what anyone back that way looked like, though."

Madsen said, "I can tell you what one of 'em looked like. We got him on ice at the morgue. He was an Indian agent who liked ragtime. That makes his killing federal. Now all we got to find out is who the *other* cuss was. For some reason none of the gents back near the piano seem to be able to recall a thing about the son of a bitch who shot him. The Indian agent wasn't armed, by the way."

Stringer nodded and asked, "Might the dead man have answered to the name Manson?" To which the lawman answered with a frown, "Of course not, I'm Madsen, damn it."

Stringer laughed and said, "Hell, I know that, Chris. I was just talking to an Indian agent with the similar name of Manson, only he was Scotch, not Danish, see?"

Chris Madsen shrugged and said, "I don't know what nationality the agent shot in the Pronghorn was. His name was Davis. He was gunned down like a dog and we mean to hang his killer high, if and when we catch him. That can be tough when a wanted man gets away clean without a single lead to follow up on."

Stringer nodded, then brightened and said, "He was a Texan. Does that help?"

The older lawman nodded soberly and said, "It does, a heap. It lets off a mess of Indians who might have had it in for an Indian agent. It eliminates a heap of surly drunks from other parts of the country off as well. But how do you know the killer was a Texan if you say you wasn't there, MacKail?"

Stringer explained, "I told you I left when I heard trouble brewing. I never heard poor Davis say anything. But I did hear the man who was asking him not to feed another coin to the player piano mention that he was an unreconstructed rebel from Texas. That still leaves anything from a tall cow hand to a short oil field worker for you to worry about, of course."

Chris Madsen decided, "Most of the oil company roughnecks learned the trade further east than Texas. The western oil business is fairly new and the outfits try to hire experienced drillers. That Jack Holt you shot it out with in the depot was an old boy from Texas, wasn't he?"

Stringer nodded but said, "Let's not go clutching at

straws, Chris. There must be a heap of Texas folk who don't even know me and the one in the Pronghorn was after another man entire!"

The old man-hunter pondered on this in silence for a spell before he pointed out, "They sent Holt after you, by name, lest you put something in the papers they didn't want the rest of us reading. You just said you'd paid a call on the local Indian agency and that other Texan just shot an Indian agent! Don't that strike you as kind of sinister?"

Stringer shook his head and said, "The head agent I talked to had a name that sounds a lot like your own and all of us are still alive. You trip over a heap of such coincidences in my game, Chris. After a while you learn not to take them all that serious. I never met any Indian agent named Davis. So he couldn't have told me any secrets worth a man's life."

Madsen asked, "What if they were out to shut him up before he *could* tell you anything?" So Stringer said, "That's reaching for it, Chris. If the man who shot Davis was working with Jack Holt, or the same employer, how come nobody went after *me*? I was near the window, in plain view, right?"

Madsen nodded and said, "Sure you was, armed and dangerous after you'd just proved the same with another gunslick Say someone keeping an eye on you figured you was after something Davis knew. Say they knew you hadn't talked to the Indian agent they was worried about. Say they sent another hired gun into the Pronghorn after you, scared shitless, and he saw Davis was in the back, maybe to meet you in secret, and, him being unarmed and helpless, the killer went after safer game? I just don't buy a man shooting another down in cold blood over piano music, do you?"

Stringer blew a thoughtful smoke ring and observed, "Oh, I don't know. Kid Curry once bragged to me, personal, about his gunning another owlhoot just for spilling coffee on him, and they say Cockeyed Jack McCall shot James Butler Hickock in the back for no other reason than the pure hell of it. This world is full of crazy-mean bastards and they do seem to grow up a mite meaner out our way. I'd keep a more open mind on the Davis killing if I were you, Chris."

Madsen asked, "Then are you saying there can't be no connection at all betwixt the attempt on you and the success on Davis?"

Stringer shook his head and explained, "I'm saying I don't know. What tribal desk was Davis holding down before he was murdered this afternoon?"

Chris Madsen took a notebook from his shirt pocket, scanned it, and said, "Osage. Does that mean much to you?" To which Stringer could only reply, "Not yet. But it's worth keeping in mind. I seem to be on friendly terms with a member of the Osage tribal council. I might see what he has to say about any fuss they've been having with their oil leases or whatever."

Then he glanced up at the darkening sky, which was really fixing to glow red tonight, with that big fire still blazing just outside of town. He rose, saying, "It's getting sort of late to go calling on any breed of Indian. I reckon I'll go up, do some writing, and turn in, if it's all the same with the law in these parts."

Chris Madsen nodded and said, "I wish you'd do that. We got enough checkers spread out on the board as it is. Can I tell the boss you're out of the game for the night?"

Stringer said he sure could, unless the hotel caught fire. So they shook on it and Stringer went back inside.

Irene at the switch board shot him a friendly smile and looked as if she wanted him to come over and jaw some more about the outside world she found so thrilling. But he just tipped his hat brim at her and went on up to his room.

He found the door unlocked. He drew his S&W and ducked in fast, sliding his back to one side along the wall as he threw down on the only strange figure in sight. Then he noticed it was Bubbles and that she looked more tempting than strange as she reclined on his bed covers like Cleopatra reading a magazine, albeit he'd always pictured Cleopatra with just a few more clothes on.

As he shut and barred the door behind him, holstering his gun at the same time, his rival reporter smiled uncertainly up at him and said, "I was afraid you'd be mad at me, about what happened at the Western Union today, I mean."

He got rid of his hat and began to shuck the rest of his gear as he assured her, "You do have a swell way of making up for rude behavior. I wasn't sore to begin with. You beat me to the wire fair and square."

She tossed her magazine aside and lay back to unpin her blond hair as she dimpled up at him and said, "Goody. I know we did agree to share the news, here, and I did wire your paper the lead with details to follow, once I'd filed my own scoop. I do have a duty to my own paper, you know. Did you finally get your own story off, dear?"

He said, "Yep, I was wondering why the news desk seemed a mite confused, at first."

Then he sat down beside her to shuck his Justins and jeans as she asked, without real interest, "Oh? Did they wire you back more questions, then?"

He told her that was close enough and took her in his arms to get down to details they were both interested in at the moment. But as he was entering her she murmured, "Wait, there's an interesting angle I came up with earlier today." Then, as he paused, in a really ridiculous position, she sighed and said, "For God's sake, *do* it! Nothing else on earth seems half as important right now!"

So he did it, and he felt sure she was right until they'd climaxed, twice, and lay side by side in sated languor with the red glow from the window glowing on their damp naked flesh. Then he cuddled her closer and murmured, "You were saying . . . ?"

She giggled, snuggled closer, and replied, demurely, "You took the words right out of my mouth, bless you. I stepped into a beauty parlor this afternoon. You should smell the gunk they use on Indian girls to give them a fashionable curl. My waves are natural, thank you very much, but you'd be surprised how much gossip one can pick up at such an establishment while having one's nails done."

He said, "No, I wouldn't. Small town barber shops work the same way. What did you find out, aside from the fact that some Indians admire the Gibson Girl look, I mean?"

She confided, "It's not Indian girls some awful woman called Madam Pearl has been importing. They said something about a Belle Starr as well. But wasn't she the outlaw queen who was hot a few years ago?"

He said, "Yep, over near Fort Smith. She'd be proud to hear herself described as an outlaw queen. She had a daughter by the name of Pearl, too. I understand she's all grown up and running a house of ill repute in Fort Smith these days. Her daddy was Cole Younger, so that makes the results pure white and not qualified to squat in the Cherokee Strip like her late mamma."

Bubbles began to toy absently with him as she thought and decided, "Oh, I've heard about the Cherokee Strip. It's that long skinny thing sticking out the west end of this territory, right?"

He sighed and said, "That's the Oklahoma Panhandle. They just tossed it in as land unclaimed by either Texas or Colorado when they declared it all Oklahoma Territory and let the white sooners move in. As a part of the old Indian Nation, the Cherokee Strip ran along the Arkansas border to the east. Belle Starr and Cole Younger were only a few of the pests who hid out there, safe from the Cherokee Police as long as they sold moonshine cheap and confined their robberies to other parts. Federal Judge Isaac Parker of Fort Smith, Arkansas, finally cleaned up the Cherokee Strip by sending in U.S. Federal deputies and stringing up any white or reasonably white outlaws they brought back to him. I don't see what any of that could have to do with current troubles in Tulsa and I hope you notice that the long skinny thing sticking out of this particular state I'm in is getting stiffer by the stroke."

She laughed and said she noticed it wasn't all that skinny any more as she rolled atop him to impale herself on his newly inspired panhandle. So they didn't get to talk sense for another sweet while. But as she climaxed and fell down across him limply, he said, "You forgot to tell me what the other gals say Pearl Starr might be doing here in Tulsa, if it's her they're fussing about. With all the new hands in town for this oil boom, there ought to be more than enough customers to go around."

Bubbles remained atop him, throbbing pleasantly, as she yawned and said, "Oh, they never accused her and her girls of whoring for white boys. They seem out to marry up with Indians, lawsome and proper. Doesn't that sound odd, dear?"

He said, "Nope. Just shady," and went on to tell her about the white adventuress who'd taken advantage of a lovestuck drunken Indian, adding, "I doubt either one of us could get space rates on that angle. Most of our readers already know this world is infested with low lifes and those who don't are hopeless. I don't know how many times we've printed warnings about gold bricks and the suckers go right on buying 'em. I've about finished running my poor brain in the squirrel cage of BIA rules and regulation that don't seem to agree with one another. I just saw a whole bookcase of the nonsense and somehow I don't think my feature editor wants that long a feature on local color."

She began to move a mite, teasingly, as she replied, "Mine, neither. How do you feel about chipping in with me for a nice private compartment on the train to the coast? I'd feel awkward doing this in daylight behind the drapes of a Pullman berth."

He laughed up at her and said, "So would I. But who said anything about leaving for the coast right now?"

She said, "Me. We've got plenty of notes on the local color as well as the basic facts. Rude roughnecks keep whistling at me and shooting at you. So why don't we quit while we're ahead? You know neither of our papers are going to run more than four columns on Tulsa if the whole place blows up, and any writer worth his or her salt could do a full page on what we already have."

He didn't answer. Nothing seemed as important, at the time, than the heavy breathing she'd inspired on both their parts. And so, since she didn't seem up to moving her parts all that fast, Stringer rolled her on her back, hooked an elbow under both her wide-spread dimpled knees and forgot about everything else in the universe for an all-too-short lovely time.

When it was over, Bubbles gasped, "Woosh! You sure come with a lot of energy. If the killers after you aren't out to cover up Pearl Starr's matrimonial agency, what's left?"

He rolled off her, chuckling fondly, as he said, "I've heard of a nose for news, but you're something else. I don't even want to think about those Fort Smith fancy gals right now, you pretty little thing. Just let me get my second wind and I'll show you a position I'll bet you've never tried. Or would you rather save some for morning?"

She asked if they couldn't do both. So they did. Sort of. When he woke up the next morning Stringer found himself alone in bed.

CHAPTER
SIX

By the time he'd bathed, shaved and dressed himself, Stringer could tell by the street noises outside that he'd overslept a mite. It had to be pushing eight A.M. That no doubt accounted for Bubbles slipping back to her official room number, lest she be caught in the hall in broad daylight and a kimono with her hair unpinned. He considered giving her door a friendly pat on his way down to breakfast. But his boots were a bitch to slip off and on and he was hungry as a bitch wolf. So he decided to let sleeping gals lie, for now.

Downstairs, he found Irene, the pretty little breed, holding the fort alone behind the counter. The wall clock behind her told him it was a mite *after* eight, in fact. He didn't ask. It was none of his beeswax, but Irene said, "I'm filling in for Mister Kelly 'til he gets here. I get off at eight this evening."

He nodded and said, "Remind me not to wait that

long if I have any more long-distance calls to make. I hope your day-shift clerk shows up soon, so's you can at least get to sit down for twelve hours."

She shrugged and said, "Oh, I don't mind leaping from desk to switchboard. It's sort of interesting. It's after I get off at night that vexes me. I don't have any friends up here in Tulsa, and, of course, I have to go straight home, having no escort. There's a new picture show from France playing just down the street, too. They say a mess of French gals dance the can-can in it, bold as brass, too. I'd surely like to see a picture show like that. Wouldn't you?"

He smiled thinly and replied, "Right now I'd rather see a plate of ham and eggs and at least two mugs of coffee. I don't suppose you know a place where I could stuff my fool face?"

She lowered her long lashes as she murmured, "Not until I get off work, if you're talking about really fine home cooking. But you might try the cafe between here and the depot, on this side of the street."

He thanked her and was about to leave. Then he considered the feelings of Bubbles, if she ever woke up, and asked Irene if he could leave a note in the key box of that other member of the Fourth Estate, W.R. Hackman.

Irene shook her head and said, "Miss Hackman's gone. She checked out just a few minutes ago, bag and baggage."

Stringer frowned and said, "That's odd. She never mentioned moving when we, ah, met at a press conference yesterday. Did she say where she was headed?"

Irene told him, "Not in so many words. But she did say something about the 8:45 westbound. You could likely still catch up with her at the depot if it's important."

Stringer considered. Then he grinned and said, "I can't think of anything important we could accomplish in such short a time in a railroad waiting room. I'd best go see about those eggs aboard fried ham. I hope your room clerk shows up soon, Miss Irene."

She placed one finger along the side of her nose and winked at him as she confided, "He won't. She's very pretty."

Stringer laughed, ticked his hat brim at her, and left in search of the cafe she'd told him about.

It wasn't much. There were only four tables and all four were occupied. He was about to turn away when he heard his name called from a corner table and saw the two gents seated at it were Bull Durham and Tiger Twain, of all people. It was Durham who waved him over to a vacant bentwood chair. Tiger was just staring at him, thoughtfully. As Durham introduced Stringer to the driller he'd yet to meet formally, Tiger ignored the hand Stringer held out and said, "We've rubbed noses in the past. Wasn't it you I saw whispering with Lawyer Lacey just before the son of a bitch had me fired?"

Stringer sat down as he replied, easily, "I don't recall whispering about anything, Tiger. I asked him for a ride back to town, loud and clear. That was before you blew the top of that hill, I'll thank you to recall. So kindly leave me out of your feud with Sinclair Oil, and how does a man get some breakfast in this joint?"

Bull Durham bellowed for the colored waiter, who came over wary-eyed to take Stringer's order. As he headed back to the kitchen Durham turned back to Stringer and said, "I hope we ain't at feud neither, old son. I was forced to tell the law who was in the Pronghorn, yesterday, when that fight broke out in the back. I did say I was sure you had nothing to do with it, though."

Stringer nodded and replied, "I told Chris Madsen the same tale when he caught up with me last night. I failed to mention you to him. But every man does what he thinks he ought to, and since neither of us could have gunned that Indian agent, what the hell."

Bull Durham looked relieved and made small talk with Tiger until the waiter brought Stringer's ham and eggs. As he dug in he only half listened to the conversation. It was sort of dull. The friendly but foolishly windy Durham kept suggesting outfits Tiger might be able to hire on with. Stringer knew as well as Tiger that a straw boss who'd been fired for carelessly blowing up an oil well would have a tougher time than their colored waiter getting any kind of job in Tulsa right now. Stringer considered suggesting Tiger change his name for business reasons before moving on. Then it occurred to him that Twain had to be a made-up name and that the sullen cuss no doubt had to come up with a new name everywhere he drifted with his brag and fake references. So as he washed down the last of the ham and eggs with black coffee, Stringer tried to change the subject by saying, "I have to look up an Osage called Walter Bluefeather. I don't suppose either of you gents might know him?"

Tiger just scowled. Bull Durham said, "I know *of* him. He's a bad Injun. Uses his seat on the tribal council to scalp his fellow redskins head to toe. Drives into town in a big white Stanley steamer, showing off."

Stringer said, "Not no more. He says he's in the market for a gas buggy. Do you know the way to his spread, the Rocking Tipi?"

Durham frowned and said, "Sort of. It's about six or eight miles out to the north-west, on the Osage reserve. Look for the Pawhuska Post Road and follow it 'til you come to a spread too fancy for any damned Indian and, oh, yeah, there's a pipe line alongside the road and you'll see some oil derricks just this side of Blue-feathers'. A wildcatter called Tex Roberts sunk 'em just inside that fool Indian's property line."

Stringer sipped some more coffee before he asked, casually, "Do tell? That's odd. I heard it straight from Bluefeather that he does business with Standard Oil."

Bull Durham nodded and explained, "He does now. I just told you Roberts is a wildcatter. Old John D. ain't one for taking risks with his own money. That's likely why he has so much of the same. Gents like Tex Roberts enjoy the fun and occasional profit of drilling where nobody's ever drilled afore. One hell of a heap of holes turn out dry. Do a wildcatter get lucky and bring in a producing well, the big boys buy him out, see?"

Stringer asked, "What if they don't want to sell?" To which Durham replied with a weary smile, "They always do. They don't have much choice. It takes a heap of money to sink any kind of well and the wildcat-ters are always in debt for the dry ones they sink most often. Your financial obligations are just starting when you *do* strike oil. Nobody's about to buy a drop of crude in the middle of nowhere. It has to be piped to a refin-ery, through expensive pipe lines. Once it gets there, the oil trust owns all the refineries and railroad tank cars, in any case. So it's best for everyone to just sell the fool well for a heap of cash and move on, letting the big boys worry about getting it to market, see?"

Stringer nodded and said, "I do now. I assume the oil trust has to buy the oil leases the wildcatters have had to get from the property owners to begin with?"

Bull Durham shrugged and said, "I reckon. I've never worried about such paper work. I'm an oil man, not a flimflam man."

Tiger Twain growled, "You sure do talk a lot for any sort of working man," as he rose to his feet, adding, "I need some fresh air, it stinks in here," before turning from them to stalk out, muttering to himself.

Stringer smiled thinly and said, "I wonder if that parting shot was meant for you or me," to which the friendlier oil man replied, "Don't ask him, even if you catch up with him again before he leaves town. He's one tough hairpin with an uncertain disposition. I do like to talk, so it might have been me, and I just feel sorry for him."

Stringer asked why it might have been himself. So Durham sighed and said, "He does seem to feel you put in a bad word for him with Lawyer Lacey. I tried to tell him I'd have fired him, myself, if he'd blown any oil rig *I* owned to kindling wood and then set fire to it. But you might have noticed he don't take me serious. He knows I'm just another working stiff, like him. He's really got it in for what he calls the capital class. He reads a lot of that socialist shit put out by gents like Jack London."

Stringer laughed and said, "I can't wait to tell old Jack I'm a capitalist. He's not a socialist any more, by the way. Since he published *Call Of The Wild* he's been smoking fifty cent cigars and bitching about paying taxes to support all the lazy bums who just don't want to work."

Then he got up, left a dime on the table, and headed for the cashier to pay up and be on his way to visit an Osage capitalist he knew of.

• • •

Stringer hired a retired army bay and a center-fire stock saddle at the nearest livery. One of the stable hands was an Osage who gave him even clearer directions to the Rocking Tipi. He didn't seem to be sore at Walter Blue-feather for being a mite richer than he was.

As Stringer rode out of the forest of oil derricks around Tulsa he saw that, sure enough, a six-inch pipe ran along the ditch beside the prairie wagon trace to the Osage capital at Pawhuska. It lay mostly sun-baked in this kind of weather, save for where it lay half sub-merged in oily water along the bottom of a draw. The dry sea of grass all around was sort of wavy and, once he was out of town a ways the draws were timbered with cottonwood, crack willow and wild choke-cherry. The rises were not only grassy but overgrazed. He knew the Osage had been quicker to grasp the advantages of raising beef instead of hunting it than their Sioux cousins to the north. They seemed to be overdoing it on this range. But white stockmen tended to be just as bad at overstocking their range. So what the hell.

He spied the grove of oil derricks ahead and to his left long before he could get close enough to them to matter. When at last he came to the first one, he heard what sounded like the sneaky sounds of life coming from the bitty shack next to the gummed up drilling platform and reined in to call out a howdy.

There was no answer. He rode closer and laughed at himself when he realized there was nobody there but the whispering steam engine that was pumping the well. He had better luck at finding signs of life when he topped the rise beyond to rein in and admire the mighty fancy homestead facing him on the far slope. The main ranch-house rambled along the sunward slope in a manner to do any cattle baron proud. Neither the barn or attached outbuildings were anything to sneeze at, either. The only indication that the owner might be Indian was the lack of paint or whitewash on the sun-silvered planks and shingles. Stringer had no idea why Plains Indians simply refused to paint wood. He just accepted it as a notion they had as much right to as the Mexicans did blue window-shutters or his own kind's habit of growing inedible posies out front.

A whole mess of folk were seated at a trestle table in the door yard, oblivious of the glaring sun that was still on its way up in the cloudless cobalt sky. As Stringer rode in, a couple of fox-faced cur-dogs with tails to match came at him and his mount, barking threats of sure death, until a tall familiar figure rose from the table and yelled at them in Osage. That stopped the dogs in their tracks and made them head the other way, tails between their legs. Stringer admired a dog owner who didn't allow his property to act like spoiled brats. As Stringer rode closer Walter Bluefeather waved him on in and called out, "You're just in time, Paleface. We're fixing to have us some ice cream."

As Stringer dismounted a young Osage ranch hand ran over to grab his reins and lead the bay to shade and water. The Osage seated around the table seemed made of sterner stuff. They paid no attention to the cloud of hover flies above the table, either. As Bluefeather introduced Stringer to his kith and kin they turned out to be a mixed bag of men, women and children, including the ones who'd tried to run their uncle's Stanley steamer into the river the day before. Some of the gals were handsome and a couple looked at least half white. Stringer saw no sign of the white wife and in-laws Bluefeather was said to have. There was a milk bucket-sized ice cream maker on the table. As Stringer sat down with them, Bluefeather told him, "It's your turn to crank, MacKail. I don't know why the fool thing is taking so long this morning. I ordered me the best brand from Monkey Ward and we done ever'thing the instructions said. But she just won't go."

Stringer leaned foreward to give the crank on top an experimental turn. Then he said, "You're right. The makings feel thin as buttermilk. You're sure you have plenty of cracked ice and rock salt around the inner liner?"

Bluefeather frowned and said, "Sure we got ice in her. Do you take me for a noble savage? Run that part about rock salt past me again."

Stringer explained, "You're supposed to mix rock salt with the cracked ice. It makes the ice melt faster and that draws heat from your ice cream mix, see?"

Bluefeather laughed and said, "Well, I never. Somebody run in the house and ask the cook for a measure of rock salt." So six kids and four grown men jumped up to dash for the nearby house. Stringer knew kids were just like that. Rich men of any breed always had ass kissers hanging about.

As they waited for the rock salt Walter Bluefeather handed Stringer a Havana Claro and asked what might have brought him out this way, aside from a passion for home-made ice cream.

Stringer said, "I wanted to clear up a point about tribal councils, seeing as I heard you're on one. Did you hear about the runaway well in the old Creek graveyard?"

Bluefeather laughed and said, "Yeah, I wish I'd been there. Creek don't know the value of money. All they want is yaller shoes and a bottle of gin. They already got more oil wells than they need and what might a Creek graveyard have to do with the Osage council?"

Stringer said, "Nothing, direct. I was hoping you could fill me in on the difference between tribal land held in trust to the council and privately owned Indian land, like your own."

Bluefeather thumbnailed a kitchen match and lit the cigar for Stringer as he said, "That's easy. The original notion of the Great White Pappa was that each nation would get a chunk of the Indian Nation, held in common, the area depending on the head-count of the folk involved."

He shook the match out and continued, "At the same time they were trying to get us all to live white, offering us seeds, tools, scholarships to Carlisle College back East and so on. We went along with 'em, having no choice when even we could see there was just no way to live on so little hunting range the *old* ways. One farm can feed thirty families or more whilst a hunting band of say thirty needs at least a couple of hundred square miles of such dry country."

Stringer shot an admiring glance around as he said, "I can see you Osage were quick learners." To which Bluefeather replied with a nod, "Like I said, we had to be. One of the first things we learned was that old Karl Marx was full of it. You just can't work land communal. A family has to *own* land before they'll work it enough to matter. So after a while, the BIA changed the rules, they do that a lot, and allotted a section or quarter section to each family head, depending on whether he wanted to graze it or plow it. Us Osage opted mostly for grazing stock. Cherokee like farming better than we ever did. But in the end, there was land left over because the damned BIA would only give clear title to so much land to one family, see?"

Stringer nodded and said, "It could have been worse. The B.I.A. could have given the leftover land to somebody else."

Bluefeather growled, "They tried to. We took 'em to court and won. There's a lot to be said for sending Indian boys to Carlisle. Red Cloud might have hung on to the Black Hills if he'd sent a few Lakota boys back East to pick up law degrees instead of making faces at you folk. In the end, Washington had to agree that since all us civilized nations were increasing, the tribal councils could hold the extra land in trust to deal out to new families. So that's what we've been doing ever since."

Stringer nodded and asked, "In the meantime, who gets the money from oil leases on tribal lands held in trust?"

Bluefeather said, "Speaking only for the Osage, since all Cherokee are crooked and all Creek are stupid, such profits go into the Osage treasury to cover the cost of government. Then anything left over is distributed fair and square to each family head." He chuckled and added, "It's been rolling in pretty good. At the rate we're going, even the Creek will be rich without lifting a lazy finger."

Stringer shot a thoughtful glance at the distant oil derricks, still on Bluefeather's property, and said, "I can see you must have gotten rich before the oil was discovered, no offense. For didn't you just say one section was all you were supposed to own, privately, to begin with?"

A couple of kids were coming their way, proudly holding a pail of rock salt between them. Bluefeather told them to set it on the table before he told Stringer,

"I'm a good stock man and I was born blessed with a good head for business. Trade between our kind and your own is forbid by statute law lest we take advantage of you. But we're allowed to do business among ourselves, just like any other civilized folk. Show me how you make ice cream with rock salt."

Stringer half rose to do so. But as he removed the lid and some of the cracked ice to mix the salt in with it, he just had to say, "In other words, you helped yourself to land titles held by other Osage, right?"

Bluefeather chuckled fondly and said, "Hell, I paid heap big wampum for the range less hardworking stock men were starving on. What's wrong with that? Didn't the Great White Pappa order us, at gunpoint, to straighten up and act like the rest of you? Getting rich by screwing others is the American Dream, ain't it?"

Stringer had to laugh as he put the ice cream maker back together and started cranking. It was hard to interview Indians and make ice cream for them at the same time. So he didn't try and, in a little while, the contents seemed to be getting thicker and he said so. Bluefeather told Stringer to let him have a turn at the crank. Stringer didn't argue. It was hot, sweaty work and his host was welcome to the glory. The big Indian began to sweat, too, but cranked even harder as he laughed like a big kid and shouted, "Wa! It feels nice and stiff, now. Get the dishes ready, Honey. Uncle Walter is fixing to dish out some ice cream!"

Stringer didn't blame Bluefeather for calling that one gal a honey. She had a pretty face and a swell shape to go with it. As the two of them proceeded to serve the ice cream, though, Stringer was still ready to buy her as a niece or whatever until he noticed Bluefeather patting her shapely ass and making her act flustered, albeit not at all annoyed by his familiar teasing. Stringer knew most Indians felt so strongly about incest that they seldom laid hands on anyone they weren't known to be sleeping with, with the full approval of anyone who might notice. So, right, she was his full blood playpretty and where in thunder was the white wife he was supposed to have?

That was no sort of question one asked a host with his playpretty seated next to him at table, of course. So, as they all ate ice cream Stringer asked Bluefeather, casually, "How did you manage to sign an oil lease with old John D., seeing he's so pale of face these days?"

Bluefeather laughed, stuffed more ice cream in his hatchet face, and swallowed before he replied, "I told you we knew how to argue with you folk safer than our buffalo-hunting kin. We fight for our rights with lawyers. White lawyers to front for us in court and Indians with law degrees riding herd on the white boys for us. There's no sense sending a red lawyer in to argue for us in front of blue lipped federal judges who all seem to look like Andrew Jackson's kids. Chief Ross of the Cherokee found that out the hard way when he argued their case in front of the Supreme Court and they handed him some wooden cigars and told him to go stand in front of a tobacco shop."

Stringer nodded and said, "I was told as much at the BIA in town. They said you needed a white sponsor to sign legal contracts for you."

Bluefeather nodded and said, "I got one. My Indian lawyer found me a white lawyer with a poor relation I could marry up with. So that's what I done. How about a second helping?"

Stringer declined as he shot a look at the Osage gal seated next to Bluefeather almost in his lap. As if he'd read Stringer's mind, Bluefeather added, "In name only, of course. I'm sort of particular who I go to bed with. I forget the fool white woman's name. You could look it up if you want to do a story about the shameful way white folk are exploiting us."

Stringer laughed and said, "I really feel sorry for you. Anyone can see that someone is sure exploiting someone else in these parts. I fear they may have overdone it when they got you boys to settle down and behave like white folk."

As he was riding back to town Stringer could see the Biblical pillar of fire rising from the old Creek graveyard over the horizon. The rest of the sky was still clear and the sun was straight overhead, now. He slipped off his denim jacket and looped it through the thongs that would be holding the throw rope if he was using this saddle serious. It helped a mite. But the Oklahoma sun still sucked sweat through his hickory shirt as he loped along under it.

From time to time he passed one of Bluefeather's cows, even though he was well off the Rocking Tipi by now. The brand was easy enough to read, once you knew it was supposed to be a rocking tipi instead of a misshapen X with an inverted arc under it. Stringer assumed this was open range, whether owned by the federal government or tribal council. All range and reservation land was supervised by the Interior Department when you got right down to it. Stringer chuckled as he considered all the land-use loop holes folk of every complexion came up with this far from Washington. He was trying to recall the name of that California cattle baron who'd had himself carried in a row boat in order to be able to swear under oath he'd crossed all that bone-dry grass by *boat*, seasonal swamps being a heap cheaper to pay yearly grazing fees on. Then he reined in on a rise to contemplate the chongo-horned critter staring up at him, just this side of the tanglewood along the bottom of the draw ahead. He told his old army mount, "That looks like a range queer to me, old gal," and then, as the brute pawed dust and lowered its head Stringer added, "No doubt about it. He's surely out to kill me and screw you, or vice versa."

Range queers were like that. A bull calf left uncut grew up to charge anything afoot and mount any cow in heat. One cut right grew up to take no interest in anything but getting fat. But every now and again they cut a steer wrong and the results were a queer critter with mixed-up instincts. It didn't really know how to mate with a cow. But it felt it ought to at least try and mate with something, be it a cow, another steer, a pony or, hell, a tumbleweed if only it would hold still.

So as the range queer headed their way, bawling love songs or threats, it was hard to tell, Stringer nodded and spurred his mount toward it, at first, then reined sharp right to cut inside the circle of its charge. As he did so a rifle squibbed in the brush beyond and Stringer yelled, "Aim at *him*, not *us*!" as the bullet hummed past too close for comfort.

The unseen rifleman fired again and this time Stringer knew for sure who the intended target was. It was not the demented longhorn. So Stringer drew his six-gun and hung down the far side of his mount, Comanche style, as he rode for the same bush cover.

It almost worked. They were most of the way down the slope when Stringer felt the wet smack of his mount taking a rifle round and let go the horn to land running as the old bay dove ass-over-tea-kettle into some sun-flower stalks and just lay there.

Another round showered Stringer with chewed-up cottonwood bark as he made the cover of the draw and crouched behind a tree trunk, searching for the source of his discomfort. He could see perhaps five yards into the tangle of twigs and fluttering leaves. He was mad as hell, but he kept his thoughts to himself as he waited and wondered. Sometimes a bushwhacker was dumb enough to move in for a look-see after a man he'd fired on dropped out of sight and lay doggo.

But this, apparently, was not to be such a time. He heard the hoof-beats of a pony departing for other parts in a hurry. He doubted he was listening to the poor brute he'd just been riding. After a time a redbird crapped on his hat from a limb above him. He didn't comment on that, either. His poor hat was already a mess and everyone knew that when there were two bad apples in the barrel, one might ride off and leave his pard in place to see if they could sucker a greenhorn.

But by the time the whole tangle had come back to life, with birds tweeting and squirrels scampering about as if he was just an old stump, Stringer decided he was likely alone down here after all.

He didn't take that for granted. He eased to the far side of the draw and had a peek up the barren slope to the south. He saw no ponies tethered there. He still moved in slow and quiet as a Cheyenne stealing horses from a Crow camp until, at last, he'd made sure there'd only been one bushwhacker and that the yellow-bellied son of a bitch had lit out as soon as the fight seemed less than halfway even. Muttering, "Shee-it! He had a rifle against a bitty .38 and he still ran off, the heroic bastard!" as he made his way to where he'd last seen his hired mount. When he found it in the weeds he was saddened to see it was still alive, lying gut-shot amid the sunflowers as it stared up at him like a hurt pup, with trusting eyes.

Stringer soothed, "Easy, Brownie. I've always been on your side. You know that, don't you?"

The shot-up bay seemed to take some comfort from Stringer's gentle tone. It snorted and lay its head down in the tangled fuzzy stalks. Stringer hunkered down, took hold the bridle with his left hand to hold the big head steady, then placed the muzzle of his six-gun to the depression over the bay's sad left eye and fired. The hurt brute went stiff all over, and lay still.

Stringer hauled his jacket clear and put it back on. Then he reloaded his sidearm and put it back on its holster, as he muttered, "We'll both pay for this, old gal. I'm out the deposit I left at your livery, and the son of a bitch who shot you figures to pay in blood if I can prove what I'm starting to suspect." Then he headed on to town, the hard way.

CHAPTER
SEVEN

They were pretty good sports about it at the livery, albeit they charged him for the saddle whether they got it
back or not when they sent out the buckboard to salvage
the hide as well.

After such a hike under a hot sun Stringer needed to
wet his whistle before he did anything else. So he
headed for the nearest saloon and, as luck would have
it, this turned out to be the Pronghorn again.

He didn't care. He ordered a schooner of draft and
carried it back toward the player piano to sit down. The
place was almost empty, and nobody had put a coin in
the piano. So it was almost ominously quiet when
Stringer sat down across a table from Tiger Twain and
said, "I'm glad you're here, Tiger. It saves me traipsing
all over town after you on such a warm day."

Tiger frowned uncertainly and asked, "Why would

you be looking for me, MacKail? I got nothing to say to the likes of you."

Stringer made sure he had the beer schooner handle in his right hand and kept an eye on Tiger as he inhaled some suds. Then he lowered his drink and said, wistfully, "You just don't like to take chances, do you?"

Tiger muttered, "I don't know what you're talking about and, by the way, I'm not armed."

Stringer rose high enough to see that was true. Then he got up all the way and unbuckled his gun rig. He hung it by the buckle from a nail driven into the wall with hats in mind. Then he smiled wolfishly down at Tiger, saying, "I'm not armed, either, and sure you know what I'm talking about, you sneaky bit of stockshooting shit."

Tiger Twain got slowly to his own feet, stepping clear of the table as he softly growled, "I don't much enjoy being called a shit, little darling."

The quiet but ominous exchange had not been lost on the few other patrons. So as the barkeep took the one big mirror down from the wall, the Pronghorn commenced to empty, fast.

Tiger Twain told Stringer, "We seem to have the place to ourselves of a sudden. So it won't shame you if you'd like to swallow some words, or at least explain 'em afore I tear your face off, MacKail."

Stringer said, "I might have been too hasty in describing you as shit. I've yet to be bushwacked by a turd. How do you feel about yellow-bellied mammy jammer?"

Tiger Twain must not have liked it. For he threw a roundhouse right that might have killed Stringer if it had landed. But the somewhat leaner Stringer blocked the sucker punch with his left forearm and counter-punched with a right cross that busted Tiger's lip, ruined his toothy smile forever, and sent him crashing to the floor, blubbering that he'd been kilt.

Stringer snarled, "Get up and fight, you bastard. I'm not half done with you, yet."

So, after some consideration, Tiger rolled out of easy kicking range and got back up, with a six-inch boot knife in his hand.

Stringer snatched his unfinished beer from the table he was closer to, tossed the contents in Tiger's face, and smashed the glass schooner on the corner of the table to face the knife with the wickedly sharp if shorter result.

Then a voice behind him said, mildly but firmly, "That's enough, MacKail. I'm not going to say that twice."

Stringer glanced over his shoulder to see U.S. Deputy Bill Tilghman and a meaner-faced back-up in the blue uniform of the Indian Police on duty in the otherwise empty saloon. Neither had drawn his sidearm. But both were heeled with government issue Colt .45s. So Stringer dropped the busted beer schooner and muttered, "Spoilsport. This was just commencing to get interesting."

Tilghman nodded curtly and said, "We noticed. They just told us at the livery acoss the way that you'd walked into town all dusty and pissed, with the stated intent of killing somebody. I can't let you do that, old son. This ain't Dodge in the bad old days and, even when I did pack a badge in Dodge, I thought it my duty to keep things civilized. So I'll tell you what I think we'd best do."

Tilghman smiled grimly at Tiger Twain, whose knife had by this time vanished as if by magic, and said, "Mister Twain, we have a vagrancy ordinance in Tulsa and you have neither a job nor the hope in hell of ever getting one in these parts after what you done with high explosives yesterday."

Tilghman indicated the Indian at his side and added, "This here is Officer Jake Wetumpka of the Creek Nation. He's going to escort you down to the depot now, and make sure nobody hurts you until the next eastbound pulls in. Be on it when it pulls out. Do we understand each other?"

Tiger wiped the back of a hand across his bleeding mouth and protested, "You can't run me out of town, damn it! It was MacKail as started it. I ain't done nothing to deserve such cruel and unusual punishment!"

Tilghman chuckled fondly and said, "Sure you have. A heap of Creek a e sore at you as well. They were sort of counting on that oil money that's still going up in smoke, even as we speak. I'm a peace officer, not a judge. My job is to keep the peace and I don't see how I'm going to do that as long as you are still in town. So I'm ordering you to leave. It's as simple as that."

Tiger protested, "What about MacKail? He's the one as come in here calling me mean names!" to which the older lawman replied, gently but firmly, "I mean to chide *him* about his manners as well. Jake, take Mister Twain to the depot and see that he gets off safely, hear?"

The younger lawman grinned ferociously and asked, "Do I get to gun him if he won't get on the train, Bill?"

Tilghman replied, "I feel sure he'll get on the train. But you just do whatever you have to, old son."

So Wetumpka frog-marched the battered Tiger out the front door as Tilghman moved to the bar, peered over it, and asked the barkeep to get off the floor and produce a couple of cold beers. When the rattled barkeep had done so, Tilghman moved the schooners and

Stringer to the nearest table and said, "Sit down, old son. You and me had best have a talk."

Once they were both seated, with suds to sip, Tilghman said, "You go off half-cocked like that again, I'll have to charge *you* with vagrancy, too, even if you do have visible means of support. Your place of employment ain't in Oklahoma, if you follow my drift."

Stringer protested, "That son of a bitch just tried to kill me and he *did* kill my *pony*, Bill! You can't just let him *go*!"

Tilghman swallowed some beer, lowered his schooner to the table, and replied, "I just did. They told me at the livery about what happened. You was shot at by a person or persons unknown on the way back from the Rocking Tipi. I see now who you suspected done the deed, and I'm glad I caught up with you afore anyone was hurt serious. You don't have a shred of evidence as would hold up in court and, had you killed him, I don't see how you'd ever get off on less than manslaughter."

Stringer protested, "It had to be him. Hardly another soul in town knew I was riding out to Walter Bluefeathers' and he was the only one who said right out that I stunk. He seems to have thought I had something to do with his getting fired. It seems obvious he had the motive, saw the opportunity, and lay for me out on the range to nail me in private."

Bill Tilghman inhaled some more suds before he shook his head wearily and said, "You can't kill a man or even arrest him for a *seem*, old son. I'll allow he's an unpleasant asshole. But how much peace would I be able to keep around here if half the assholes in Tulsa was slaughtered just for being surly? Whether he was the one or not, he'll be gone any minute and you won't have to worry about him no more, see?"

Stringer pointed at the nearby player piano to ask, "Has it occurred to you that I found Tiger Twain drinking here and that Indian agent was gunned right there by a growly cuss who must drink here often enough to have pals who covered up for him?"

Tilghman nodded and said, "It has. Tiger Twain was up on that hill destroying oil wells at the time of the killing. He talks more Ohio Valley than Texas as well. As to the killer being a regular whose pals covered up for him, that need not be the answer. Davis drank here regular. The cuss who gunned him needn't have. Clay Allison used to gun gents in saloons regular and just walk away, leaving no witnesses who wanted to testify against him. He wasn't popular. He just scared the wits out of calmer gents. It takes guts as well as a good reason to face a killer in court and point him out as a man worth hanging. There's always the chance that he'll get off and, even if he don't get off, he might have friends just as mean. The death of Davis has all the earmarks of a paid assassination. The discussion of his musical tastes being just the excuse some such bastards seem to feel they need. Had the killer been just a nasty drunk, the boys might not have felt so shy about discussing him. In any event, Tiger Twain don't work as the one who gunned Davis, and if he was after you he ain't no more. So what are we arguing about?"

Stringer insisted, "Before I was so rudely interrupted, I had plans to beat some answers out of him. I know he wasn't the one who tried to kill me the first night I got here, and the late Jack Holt has a pretty good alibi for what happened out on the range today. If Tiger didn't gun Davis that means there's a *gang* of them and, damn it, we could still catch up with the one we know of at the depot!"

Tilghman shook his head and said, "He'd deny it, whether you're right or wrong, and beating confessions out of a man ain't my style. It's been my experience that if you pain most anyone enough, they'll confess most anything. I've always considered the Salem Witch Trials mighty poor criminal investigation. I likes to have some solid evidence afore I haul an old lady afore a judge and jury on the charge of riding on broomsticks. It's easier to run such pests out of town."

Stringer had calmed down enough by now to grin sheepishly and say, "You know, I once wrote an exposé on a sheriff who used brutal methods. But how many arrests do you get to make as such a gentle cuss, Bill?"

Tilghman shrugged and said, "Not many. Like I said, I consider myself a peace officer, with the sworn duty to keep the peace. I ain't out to get famous as a town tamer. That's likely why I never gunned my own deputy by mistake, the way old Bill Hickok did that time."

He sipped some more beer before he added, modestly, "I've never been one for gunning drunk and disorderly cow hands. I done what I had to when Judge Parker ordered me, old Chris Madsen and Heck Thomas to clean up the Cherokee Strip. In the end, we brung in over three hundred killers and Judge Parker had to sentence about half of 'em to hang, of which only eighty-eight really got to do the rope dance, the higher courts being even more gentle than we was. Some of the old boys we brung in are still with us, considerably reformed. There's nothing like a few nights staring out through the bars at the gallows to reform a wayward youth."

He finished his beer, put the empty glass firmly down, and added, "Don't make me have to calm *you* down that way, old son. Sometimes, when they say they're going to hang you, they really *do* it. It ain't a dignified way for a man to die, even if they get it right and snap your neck the first time they drop you."

Stringer grimaced and said, "I've covered a few public hangings. I'll try to be careful about going after the wrong man and, if I mess up, maybe you'll be kind enough to just shoot me, Bill."

Tilghman shook his head morosely and said, "I don't consider that professional. I pride myself on bringing my killers in alive. So just don't kill nobody unless you're damned sure you can prove self-defense and we'll say no more about it."

An hour later even Stringer felt he might have been hasty in accusing Tiger Twain, albeit he was damned if he could see who *else* it might have been. Bluefeather hadn't known he was on his way out until he'd gotten there. There were no telephone lines following the wagon trace out to the Rocking Tipi, even if the friendly Osage had something to hide. The hands at the livery had known where he was going, but they hadn't seemed to mind until he came back without their livery mount or saddle. Nobody else had known where he was going, save for old Bull Durham, and he made less sense as a suspect than Walter Bluefeather. In either case, he hadn't found out anything either man could possibly want him not to know. So it kept boiling down to Tiger, but, yeah, it could have been just a killing grudge on the part of a man who'd proven he could be reckless as well as nasty. So there was a good chance Tiger *had* been acting on his own and, if so, it was over.

He was headed for his hotel, meaning to ask Irene if there was any way to trace telephone calls between the pay phones near the depot to, say, an office or private home Jack Holt might have checked with just before that shoot-out, when he became aware of two other gents walking in step with him on either side. He'd put his .38 back on before leaving the Pronghorn, of course, but after his talk with the law he thought it best to just ask politely if there was anything he could do for them. The one on his left, who looked like a full-blood dressed like an undertaker, smiled pleasantly and said, "The lady we work for would like a word with you, MacKail."

Stringer said, "Well, I just love to talk to ladies. But does she have a name, ah, Chief?"

The Indian in the frock coat scowled and warned, "Easy on that chief shit. You can call me Hank if you have to call me anything. We'll be swinging left at the next cross street. If the lady wants to tell you her name she will. If she decides she likes you, you may live. So keep your hands polite for now and talk nice to her when we get there, hear?"

Stringer assured them he'd been raised to be polite to ladies and as soon as they turned off Main Street the one on his right helped himself to Stringer's six-gun, observing, "Nice sidearm. Double action, and I see you had the grips reshaped to your fancy when they filed the front sight down for you. I'm a .44 man, myself. Do you find a .38 has all the stopping power you might need?"

Stringer explained, "If you aim right they do. A cannon ball won't do the job if you aim *wrong*."

The friendly son of a bitch who'd disarmed him chuckled and said, "I reckon that rascal you gunned in the depot the other night would agree."

Then the Indian on the other side of Stringer said, "We want to go up them stairs now."

Stringer wanted to mount the flight of steps running up the side wall of that two story frame whatever about as much as he wanted to mount the gallows Bill Tilghman had been warning him about, earlier. But as many a man before him had no doubt discovered, there were times one seemed to have no choice. So they just went on up. The Indian opened the door and shoved Stringer inside, calling out, "We got him, Cousin."

A she-male voice trilled sweetly, "In here, Cousin Henry." So they entered a well-appointed sitting room where a very pretty, if somewhat pleasantly plump, young gal was seated on a maroon plush sofa behind a silver tea service aboard a low slung rosewood table. Considering she'd just called a full-blooded Indian her cousin, she seemed mighty palefaced. Her hair was light, henna tinted, and the roots weren't any darker than her peaches and cream complexion called for. She patted the sofa beside her ample hips and said, "Sit right down beside me, Stringer MacKail. We're going to have us some tea whilst we talk. I'm Pearl Starr. You've heard of me, or at least my famous momma, of course?"

Stringer said he surely had as he did as she asked, wishing she used less perfume. The odors of violets and Darjeeling tea, while both expensive, just didn't go too well with one another.

As she poured with her pinky raised in a refined manner, the two gunslingers who'd fetched him started to leave. Pearl Starr told the one who'd disarmed him to leave the .38 on the sideboard across the room. The Indian frowned and asked, "Are you sure, Cousin Pearl?" and she smiled sweetly and said, "Do it," in a no-nonsense tone. So they did it, and left her alone with Stringer. He was too polite, and too smart, to ask if the one she called Cousin Henry could possibly be Henry

Starr, the nephew of the late Sam Starr, wanted for
everything but the common cold. She asked if he liked
cream and sugar with his tea. He said he liked his tea
and coffee neat. She dropped four lumps of sugar in her
own cup and leaned back with it, saying, "Now let's
chat. I know your rep, Stringer. They say you never
write fibs about anyone. What were you planning to
write about me and mine?"

He sipped some tea and told her, "I hadn't thought
much about it until just now, Miss Pearl. The *San Francisco Sun* only buys news that's fit to print."

She dimpled at him and said, "Naughty, naughty. I'll
allow I have some whores working for me, as my sweet
mamma had before me. But neither of us have ever
whored, *personal*. I'd just like to get my hands on that
mean writer who writ my poor old momma sold her
body as well as moonshine and livestock at the old
homestead down at Younger's Bend. I'd just scratch his
eyes out, and I want you to know that none of the gals
here in Tulsa with us are real whores, neither. So don't
you go calling them that, hear?"

He smiled down into his cup and said, "I never intended to. Some of our readers are easy to shock, and
such doings in a far away town are of little interest in
Frisco to begin with. We have plenty of wicked ladies of
our own if we wanted to run a scandal sheet. But since
you were the one who brought it up, I do have a couple
of questions you might care to answer."

She said, "Swell, I just love to get interviewed, if
only you boys wouldn't twist everything I say. My
momma never gave one interview to nobody and they
still keep calling her a bandit queen. Have you any notion how that got started, Stringer?"

He knew exactly how the legend had begun. But he

didn't think she'd want to hear about the free-lancer
who'd been getting a haircut in Fort Smith when a
townee drifted in to report someone had shot crazy old
Belle Starr at last, or that when the newspaper man had
asked who they were talking about and been told it was
an old trash-white gal shacked up with an Indian in the
peckerwoods, period, the hungry newspaperman had in-
vented Belle Starr, the beautiful bandit queen, on the
way to the telegraph office to ask for space rates. You
got paid that way according to how much newspaper
space you could manage to fill up. So the first inkling
the outside world had of Belle Starr nee Shirley had
been a humdinger. But of course a lot of other hacks had
come up with more details ever since. Stringer could see
the poor old hag's now-grown daughter liked the legend
better than reality. So he just said, "Well, they did dig
up some records of her having appeared in court a few
times for various misdeeds. Nobody ever proved your
stepfather, Sam Starr, was much more than a carefree
Cherokee given to bending the rules a mite."

Pearl Starr nodded and said, "That's what I keep trying to tell folk. *I've* never robbed a train, neither. You
say you have some other questions to ask?"

He nodded and said, "We both know how marrying
an Indian for fun and adventure with oil leases works. I
know an Osage who told me he'd made such a marriage
of convenience with a white gal. Not trying to judge the
rights or wrongs of such a deal, I was wondering if any
of the ladies you've been dealing with might be calling
herself Mrs. Walter Bluefeather at the moment."

The young madam reached for a little black book on
the nearby lamp table, cracked it open, and scanned
through it as she read off, half to herself, "Let's see,
now. There's Mrs. Rogers, Moody, Scraper, Duck, all

married to Cherokee. Then there's the ones married to Creek gents answering to Patsalinga, Pasgaloosa, Shawmut and Oswasa. Creek like to stick to original Muskogee names, not having as much white blood. I don't see anyone married off Osage. Are you saying someone else is in the same business as us? That might account for it, and they say them Osage have a lot of oil under their range, too!"

He said, "I'm sure more than one lawyer working with the wildcatters knows a gal or more he can call on to marry a rich Indian in name only. You work with a lawyer, don't you?"

She looked away and asked if he thought it looked like rain outside. He didn't press it, since he knew the answer in any case. He said, "I can see why your gals find it so easy to fall in love with gents of the Creek persuasion. Most of Tulsa lies above Creek claims." To which she answered, primly, "In name only, as you said. I don't know much about Osage but the Cherokee are almost white and you know what they say the *Creek* are, don't you?"

He nodded but said, "The Creek I've seen here in Tulsa look no more colored than any other breed or full blood, Miss Pearl."

She shrugged and said, "Don't never say that to Cousin Henry. He likes to brag that Chief John Ross was almost a Scotchman."

He smiled thinly and said, "I wonder what Chief Mackintosh of the Creek might have been. I thought it was the Seminole who took in runaway slaves the most in the old days."

She shrugged and said, "Them, too. They all talk Muskogee so they're all the same to me and I'll have you know my daddy Cole Younger, rode for the *South*. My mamma's daddy was a judge from the South as well."

He didn't argue. He could see that her father had been white, whoever he might have been, and it was poor old Cole Younger, not him, who kept threatening libel suits about that particular detail of the legend of Belle Starr. Pearl Starr's family tree was of no concern to him or his readers. So he just nodded and said, "The important point is that since none of your gals married any Osage or half the Creek and Cherokee dealing with the oil trust, there could be any number of folk in the business of sponsoring Indian in-laws and to tell the truth that might not be it."

She asked what might be what and he explained the troubles he'd been having since he got to Tulsa. As a born plotter, she decided, after some thought, that Bill Tilghman could be right. She said, "You *got* the one you know was after you for a fact, and the one who might have just been sore at you has been run out of town."

He asked, "Then why did someone murder an Indian agent just after I'd been asking questions at the BIA?" to which she answered with a knowing smile, "Hell, nobody likes Indian agents! Didn't they run me and my poor mamma's other white kids off our dear old home-stead in the Indian Nation once our last Indian step-daddy lit out? The BIA is always messing in things that's none of its durned business. That agent they shot could have been up to most anything mean. Have any such agents you know *personal* been gunned?"

He sighed and said, "You may have a point. I don't want any more tea, Miss Pearl. Was there anything else you wanted to talk to me about?"

She said, "Not about what you're up to in Tulsa, as long as you don't intend to write mean things about me and my girls. But would you like to earn a thousand dollars? That's my long standing offer to any man who can tell me who shot my mamma in the back that time, and they do say you're good at digging up such facts."

He stared at her incredulously and replied, "I'd have to be to solve your mother's murder at this late date! No offense, but wasn't she shot a dozen or more years back, and didn't a lot of folk agree at the time that she'd likely been shot by a jealous Cherokee whose name escapes me at the moment?"

She nodded and said, "Blue Duck was his name. He swore to us that he never shot mamma, and the law couldn't pin it on him, neither. A dark mysterious stranger had been seen lurking about just afore momma was found dying on the wagon trace. He was a white man. So what was he doing in the Strip in the first place and where did he go, afterwards?"

Stringer replied that he just couldn't say. So Pearl Starr said, "Momma's last words, as she lay dying, were something like, 'Whoever would have thought it.' I've always figured she meant she was surprised at who'd killed her. That lets Blue Duck off. He was mean as hell. Wasn't there a dark mysterious stranger killing lots of women in London about the same time?"

Stringer managed not to laugh as he replied, "Jack The Ripper murdering Belle Starr would be a headline indeed, coast to coast." He was too polite to add that only the choice of victims on opposite sides of the ocean made it remotely possible. He said, "I'll study on your offer, Miss Pearl. But I can't promise anything at this late date."

She nodded and said, "Good. It's been nice talking to you, then. You'll want to reload your gun before you put it back in its holster."

He rose uncertainly, and stepped over to the side-board to pick up his .38. He checked and, sure enough, they'd removed every round in the cylinder before leaving it there so temptingly. He grinned down at her and said, "You were testing me, I see."

She coyly hauled up her skirts, allowing him to see the whore-pistol strapped to one shapely calf, as she giggled and said, "A girl can't be too careful. But I reckon I can trust you. Do you trust me?"

He assured her he did as he hastily reloaded with fresh rounds from his cartridge loops and let himself out. He trusted her about as far as he could trust any other habitual criminal. But that would have been neither polite nor wise to say.

He saw nothing of the two men who'd grabbed him off the street to interview the sassy young madam, so he made for the exit to the outside steps while the going still seemed to be good. The space between his shoulder blades tingled all the way down the stairs and he didn't feel halfway safe until he was back on Main Street. After that he just got to wonder what that had really been all about. Pearl Starr hadn't told him a thing that didn't seem to be common knowledge and he'd be switched if he could think of a thing he'd told her that could be any use to crooks. He decided to take the odd conversation at face value for now. For, if anyone connected with her gang was after him he'd been treated mighty gentle just now. Two grown men, one a known killer, had had the drop on him and only invited him to tea. If she'd put anything but tea in his cup he'd know it any minute, now. So far, he felt just swell.

He went on to his hotel to find Irene still running the place all by herself. As he leaned on the counter to jaw with the pretty part Comanche he didn't get into Osage ice cream or Cherokee gunslingers. He said, "Seeing you know more than me about telephones, I've been wondering if there was a way for a gent to make a telephone call, late at night, over by the railroad depot."

She told him there was no doubt a pay phone or two in and about the depot. He nodded and said, "I figured there might be. Is there any way to find out if someone made a late night call, and to whom, just around the time a certain train pulled in?"

She frowned thoughtfully and said, "Not from me. Nobody could have called anyone here at the hotel after eight, because that's when I shut the switchboard down for the night."

He questioned her in more detail to learn that her switchboard and all the other lines in Tulsa ran directly to Tulsa Central, meaning a second story office manned or, rather, womanned by a half dozen gals employed by the Bell Telephone Company. Anyone wanting to call anyone else in town had to give the wanted number to an operator at Central who in turn plugged it in on a switchboard much like Irene's, only bigger.

He asked if the gals at Central kept records of the calls they put through. She shook her head and said, "Heavens, why would they bother to do that? Unless it's a long distance call, like you made all the way to San Francisco, they just make the connection, listen in long enough to see they got the party you wanted, and go on to the next call. It's not like it is here, over to Central. Those girls are plugging in and plugging out like Navajo women weaving blankets. What numbers are we talking about, anyway?"

He sighed and said, "That's what I was in hopes of finding out. I can't even say for sure that Jack Holt ever made such a call. But if he did that late at night, wouldn't it be at least possible some night shift operator might remember? He had a mighty rough way of talking and they can't handle that many pay phone calls close to midnight, right?"

She looked dubious as she said, "It wouldn't hurt to ask, I reckon. I know just one or two of the girls at Central and we could drop by to ask, later tonight."

He said, "Swell. What time did you have in mind?" to which she replied, coyly, "Well, the ones you'd want to talk to don't come on until around midnight. That gives us plenty of time to take in that French picture show I told you about, after I get off this evening."

CHAPTER
EIGHT

"That was lovely. Could we do it again?" asked the pretty little breed as Stringer rolled off her, gasping for breath and fumbling for his shirt in the darkness of her bedroom on the unfashionable side of the Arkansas. He assured her he'd be proud to try as soon as he had a smoke and got his second wind. The Pathe picture show from France had been more informative than the sleepy-eyed operators Irene knew at Tulsa Central. It had been Irene's notion to cook a late supper for him after he'd had no luck at discovering the telephone number of any-body Jack Holt might have been working for. What had happened after that had been sort of mutual, even if she had sobbed, just before he'd entered her for the first time, that she wasn't that sort of gal, and what did he mean by hauling her pantaloons off like that just after she'd hauled him into her bedroom, durn it?

Some women were like that, he knew, as he rolled a

smoke while Irene got rid of the shimmy shirt she'd been screwing in, saying he'd gotten it all wrinkled, shoving it up above her breasts like that. As he struck a light he saw she looked as swell as she felt in the dark, the match light glowing on her shapely tawny torso as she regarded him with her big sloe eyes and murmured, "Oh, Lordy, did I really have all that inside me, just now?"

He shook out the match and enjoyed a drag of Bull Durham as she fumbled for the object of her adoration in the dark and gave it a playful tweak, saying, "My, it's not really half as big as it was before. Can you boys make them things get soft and hard at will?"

He said, "Alas, no. But you're doing just fine, only be careful with those fingernails, honey."

She got a better, albeit softer grasp of the situation and shyly asked him, even as she was fondling him with practiced skill, if he minded her being just an inexperienced country girl, adding, "I mean, you being used to going out with famous San Francisco opera stars and such."

He chuckled and said, "I hate to disillusion you, Irene. But hardly any famous ladies I get to interview ever seem to want to show me their new bed spreads. So I like country gals just fine."

She began to jerk him faster as she felt it rising to the occasion. But her voice was pouty as she said, "I'll bet. What about that famous blond newspaper gal at the hotel, last night? Are you saying there was nothing like this going on between you, or that you don't miss her fair white body right this minute?"

He laughed and told her, truthfully enough, "Miss Hackman was the farthest thing from my mind until you brought it up. Bring it up a little more and I'll get rid of this smoke and prove it to you."

So she did and he did and after they'd somehow wound up climaxing together on the rug, with her on top, she kissed him in a smug possessive way and announced, "I told Mister Kelly he was full of it. No mortal man could have just treated me so fine if he'd been with another gal within a week! Let's get back up on the bed and do it some more. How come you didn't want to mess with that blonde white gal, Lover Man? Is that why she checked out in such a huff?"

He helped her back into bed as he said, "I didn't know she left in a huff. I figured she had all the local color she needed and was out to scoop me."

As they snuggled down together atop the rumpled bed covers Irene asked, "What does that mean? How does a woman scoop a man? It sounds sort of dirty. Is it fun?"

He laughed and explained the meaning of the term. Irene said, "Oh, I thought there was something I'd missed. Do you think them French gals in that picture show we saw tonight do wild and dirty French things?"

He laughed and said, "Not in front of the camera, though I have seen French post cards that were a mite more shocking than any can-can dance."

She said, "Me, too. Do you men like it when gals let you put it betwixt their lips like that?" So he replied, cautiously, "I don't imagine it would hurt too much. You sure are a curious little thing, Irene."

She said, "Well, I got a right to be curious, never having been nowhere or done nothing thrilling. You've already shamed me just awful. So as long as I'm ruint in your eyes I may as well find out what all the fuss is about. I don't see what them French gals get out of being so wicked, but I mean to try everything at least once afore I die."

He didn't argue. She'd obviously played the French horn before as well, he could tell, as he just lay back and enjoyed it. For he'd felt sure, until just now, he was about finished for the night. The hot-natured little breed took a lot out of a man just doing things the old-fashioned way. But as her pursed lips began to inspire him to new heights, Stringer had to allow there was a lot to be said for French ways. It had been a French philosopher, bless him, who'd said never to make love in the morning because you never knew who you might meet at lunch. Had not old Bubbles slipped out of bed that morning without waking him, he'd no doubt have been unable to get it up again right now, with or without a French lesson. But since she had, he could, and Irene was mighty pleased when he said, "Enough of this antipasto, Sweet Lips. Let's get back to the main course."

As they did she moaned in pleasure and purred, "I see why French gals do that, now. Does this mean you'll be taking me back to Frisco with you?" To which he could only reply, with a groan, "Jesus, can't we wait for sunrise before we talk about cold gray dawns?"

The next day didn't dawn all that cold and gray. They made love before and after breakfast in bed. Then they enjoyed a nice hot bath together in tepid water before she insisted she just had to get dressed and go to work. As she sat nude on the bed to roll her stockings she did shoot him a wistful little smile and make a remark to the effect that if she wasn't ever going to see the Golden Gate she'd best hang on to her job. She said nothing else to make him feel guilty, putting her a cut above most she-males at such times.

He escorted her most of the way back to the Osage Inn, but saw her point when she remarked it might be best if she showed up alone, lest Mister Kelly surprise the world by being on duty behind the desk on time.

Stringer was thus thrown to his own devices, neither hungry nor hard-up just as downtown Tulsa was opening up for business. He started to turn in at the telegraph office, realized he had nothing to write his paper that was worth a nickel a word, and leaned against an awning post to roll a smoke as he contemplated what he might do next.

He'd just lit the smoke when a familiar blue-uniformed figure joined him there to murmur, "Morning. Nice day so far, but we sure could use some rain."

It was Officer Jake Wetumpka of the Creek Police. He looked rather pleased with himself this morning. Stringer asked, "Did you get Tiger Twain off all right, Jake?" and the young Creek laughed and replied, "Didn't we ever. I wired ahead to Fort Smith to make sure he didn't get off still inside the territory. The Arkansas Law took him off the train and out of our hair at the Missouri Pacific Depot when the eastbound stopped there. Seems he skipped bail in Little Rock about this time last year."

Stringer whistled and said, "Then he *was* a crook as well as a piss-poor oil man!" to hear Wetumpka reply, "He was working here under false colors. The real Tiger Twain got killed in the Ohio oil fields a year or so back. The one you met here admits, under pressure, that his real name's Brown. I sort of doubt that, too. But, as Brown, he owes a debt to Arkansas Society for selling bogus oil stock. Knowing just enough about the business to sell himself as an honest working man, he tells suckers he draws part of his pay in oil stock and allows he'd rather have a mite more drinking money. So the suckers think they're skinning *him*, all the while he's skinning *them* with worthless paper."

Stringer whistled and said, "He never struck me as a slicker. But, then, I reckon he wasn't supposed to. How do you suppose he slickered Sinclair Oil into hiring him as a straw boss if he was just a fake driller?"

The young Creek lawman shrugged and said, "The real Tiger Twain enjoyed a rep for knowing what he was doing. Playing boss is easier than doing the real work. Can we get outten this sun if you want to jaw, Stringer? The Sunflower, across the way, serves pretty good draft as well as shade."

Stringer didn't argue. But as they crossed the street together, he couldn't help asking if they'd suspended the rules against serving firewater to savages, now that Oklahoma was a territory instead of a glorified reservation.

Wetumpka chuckled and said, "Not hardly. That fool law is federal. But who's going to arrest me for drinking? You?"

Stringer assured the Indian he'd always thought it a fool law as well. So they went on into the Sunflower, laid out much like the more notorious Pronghorn albeit empty at this hour, and the bar maid greeted them with, "Two draft lagers coming up," as if she'd met Jake Wetumpka somewhere before.

As the two men clinked beer schooners the plump dishwater-blonde stayed with them, resting her considerable weight on the bar with her dimpled elbows. There was nothing polite either man could do about it and Stringer didn't know any secrets worth a murder in any case. So he mused, half to himself, "Twain, Brown, or whoever must have had a reason for working for Sinclair, no matter who they thought he was. He was risking exposure long before he gave himself away as an incompetent, you know."

The Indian shrugged and said, "It still made a good cover for a man on the run with the habit of letting suckers diddle him out of bogus oil stock. I don't know a thing about setting up an oil well. But, if I had to, and they'd put me in charge, I reckon I could manage. I'd just tell my crew to get to work and stand over 'em sort of officious."

Stringer inhaled some suds and decided, "I rode for a trail boss like that, one time. We'd have never noticed if the bossy cuss hadn't fallen off his pony the third or fourth day. Where Tiger slipped up was showing off with nitro he didn't really know how to use. Even the company lawyer knew enough about the business to suggest they change the drill bit when they got down to stubborn rock."

Wetumpka nodded knowingly and said, "A real driller wouldn't have got so frusterpated. Everyone knows you can drill most any place in these parts with a better than fifty-fifty chance of striking rock-oil and they allow you a few dry holes afore they fire you. We'll likely hear from the suckers he sold fake Sinclair Oil stock to in a month or so. Folk don't know they bought worthless paper until they notice they don't seem to be getting any dividends in the mail."

Stringer grimaced and said, "I can't hang around that long. I would have left by now if I hadn't been offered a whiff of gunsmoke hinting at a more important story than this oil boom."

He had another sip and added, "I've been running here and dashing there in hopes of scouting sign, but I suspect I've been going about it wrong. I hate paper cuts on my fingers, but since I doubt anyone's going to just up and tell me what they're out to hide, I'm going to have to look it up. Where would you start pawing through the files if you were me, Jake?"

The Indian shrugged and replied, "Depends on what I wanted to look up. Us Creek Police keep files on our own kind causing petty or serious trouble betwixt here and the Osage and Cherokee lines. U.S. Deputy Tilghman rides herd on white and intertribal trouble makers. So his records would read somewhat different."

Stringer shook his head and said, "I doubt anyone has gone to so much trouble to hide anything the law, red or white, would already have on file. I suspect it's a criminal record someone's out to *avoid*. Is there any other way for a heap of money changing hands in these parts, aside from dealing in rock-oil, I mean?"

The barmaid said, "Sure. There's moonshining and stealing. Do you recall the time the Starr gang robbed the Creek treasury, Jake?"

Wetumpka made a wry face and said, "I do. My daddy was on the force then, and he come home cussing just awful when he and the boys had to turn back at the Cherokee Line. But I suspicion old Stringer here, is talking serious money. There never was much serious money in these parts afore they sunk that first oil well a short spell back." He turned to Stringer to add, "All them big oil barons are crooks. Our very own President says so. I don't see how you aim to put old John D. in jail if Teddy Roosevelt can't, howsomever."

Stringer chuckled and said, "The oil trust wouldn't send a hired gun after a newspaper man. They'd just buy his newspaper if they wanted to shut him up. I have the story on the men big and small producing the black goo. The petty tinhorns who infest any boom are stale news and likely know it. This confusing nonsense about you Indians doing business with the oil trust by such complicated rules is new to me, as well as to most lawyers and judges, no doubt. A slicker slick enough to be taking advantage of some loopholes provided by the can of worms might not want the rest of the world to know what he or she is up to, so . . ."

"Hold on." The bar maid protested, "Who says one of us ladies is crooking Indians? Have I ever overcharged you, Jake, even when you was drunk?"

Wetumpka told her she was a good old gal and that he'd propose to her if ever he had an oil lease deal of his own to worry about. She giggled and coyly asked how much he made a year as member of the tribal force. Before Jake could get in more trouble, Stringer said, "I've found most master criminals to be male, no offense, Ma'am. But this formality of recruiting white kin in a hurry is one of the unusual angles I was talking about. I doubt my readers would be too interested in some trash gal bilking her Indian husband out of some oil money unless it was *serious* money. But I may as well round that base as long as I seem to be running in dumb circles to begin with."

He turned back to Wetumpka to ask, "Where would they keep records of such matrimonial matters, Jake? The county courthouse?"

The Indian shrugged and said, "They might, if there was such a courthouse. They've been talking about building a regular county around Tulsa, if ever we get statehood. Meanwhile, it depends on who marries up with whom. The BIA don't approve of red and white weddings, but can't do much to stop 'em. To be binding, at least on the Indian's side, his or her tribal council has to give approval. They generally do unless they know for a fact that the white's no durned good at all, or if the Indian is too young or feebleminded. It's hard to get a white minister to perform such ceremonies, as hung-up on brotherly love as most of 'em seem to be. But that's all right, we got our own churches and a copy of the wedding permit is sent to the tribal council. If me and old Mabel, here, ever marry up, the records will wind up in the Creek capital of Muskogee, down river near Fort Gibson. If she spurns me for a rich Osage they'll want to file it up north at Pawhuska. If she elopes with a Cherokee horse-thief, I think their records are kept at Tahlequah, near the Arkansas Line."

Stringer swore under his breath and said, "Now you're talking about me *riding* in circles. Wouldn't the Indian agency here in Tulsa have such records, whether they approve or not?"

The Indian said, "I can't say. I don't work for 'em, and I've given up trying to understand 'em. They keep changing the rules back and forth every election. We do our best to ignore Indian agents unless they owe us money. Do you know the rascals want to cut off government allotments to Indian families who have oil wells on their land? That infernal Teddy Roosevelt even says he hopes to see the day when we all get to vote, drink, and pay taxes like everyone else!"

He gulped a mouthful of beer and added, "We already drink as much as we need to and we can't see paying taxes at all."

Stringer chuckled and said, "At the rate you boys are going, I see a time ahead when you'll have all the privileges of a white man and we'll still be supporting you, tax free. But if we could stick to the here and now, I'll ask if they have a file on mixed marriages at the BIA. I doubt that's anything anyone is out to hide in any case. To make oil deals with Indians, even a crook would need to make that angle a matter of public record."

The barmaid suggested, "Bigamy might be worth hiding, seeing how a wicked gal could marry a Creek, an Osage and a Cherokee in turn without the bans winding up in one file."

Stringer nodded thoughtfully and said, "It sure could be *profitable*. I've been told by two different folk that nobody expects a white wife-in-name-only to live on any reservation, and a really brazen gal could hope to get away with it by changing her name each time an Indian changed her name for her."

He sipped the last of his beer and decided, "I doubt crooks brazen as that would be worried about an out of town newspaper man, though. For how could I *prove* such flummery even with all the papers spread on this very bar? There's no way I could catch the same gal in bed with three widely separated oil well Indians. I just can't see anyone dumb enough to file the same name on more than one marriage certificate. So, if there's anything on paper they're afraid I'll see, it has to be something else, and it has to be recorded right here in Tulsa. That's where they've been shooting at me, not off at some reservation headquarters."

The gal asked him if he'd like another beer. He told her he would but that he didn't have time. Then he left her flirting with Jake Wetumpka and headed for the local BIA office.

Along the way he spied a brand new Buick buckboard, painted ivory white and parked in front of the Pronghorn Saloon. He stuck his head through the bat wings just long enough to see the place was almost deserted, save for the barkeep and a red-nosed old bum who looked neither prosperous nor strong enough to crank a Buick. The barkeep was staring at him, too. So

Stringer asked, "Might Walter Bluefeather be in the back?" to which the surly barkeerp replied, "Nope. Didn't know he was in town."

Stringer thanked him anyway, and ducked back outside. There was no law saying only a rich Osage was allowed to buy a brand-new gas buggy, even a white one. But Bluefeather's Stanley had been that same shade of ivory and he had said he meant to buy a new Panard or Buick. Stringer strode on until he came to a smaller doorway leading up to the offices on the top floors of the business block. He read the name plates over the mail slots just inside. He blinked and muttered, "Now, that's sort of interesting." as he made out "James Lacey, Attorney at Law."

Then he strode on. There was no proof that parked Buick back there belonged to Walter Bluefeather and, even if it did, there were other offices above the Osage might have gone up to. But Lacey did seem to be the only lawyer above the Pronghorn and old Walter had said he had a white lawyer. If Lacey was a local lawyer on retainer to Sinclair Oil, there was no reason he might not deal with local clients on the side. So Stringer told himself that even if he was guessing right instead of building mountains out of molehills, there was nothing wrong with Bluefeather having Lacey as his lawyer.

Then he stopped to get his bearings as he rolled another smoke, muttering, "Bullshit. There's a conflict of interests if Sinclair Oil hired Lacey to look after their interests here, and he made a deal for another client with Standard Oil. Bluefeather said his lawyer was his brother-in-law as well. So just what the hell is going on, here?"

He didn't want to go all the way back to the hotel. So he lit up and moved on until he spied a door sign that

contained the blue bell of the telephone company. He
entered the dinky drug store and ordered a Coca Cola at
the marble counter before he asked the old gent in
charge if he could have a look at their Tulsa telephone
directory. The old man brought it to him. So he got to
smoke, sip soda through a straw, and look up Lacey's
home address at the same time. He saw it was a good
ten blocks away. Close enough to walk, but not close
enough for Lacey to be apt to stroll home for lunch from
his office over the Pronghorn.

The half-mile hike from the drug store to the Lacey
home on a dusty street that would be tree shaded once
those spindly elm saplings grew up gave Stringer time
to think up and discard a dozen lines of bullshit. He
doubted he could pass for a Fuller Brush man or a fire
inspector in his faded denims and oil spotted Stetson,
even if he got rid of his gun rig. So when he strode up
on the porch of the mustard-painted three story house he
just twisted the door bell bold as brass and when a
sleepy-eyed young red-haired gal wearing a bathrobe
came to the door he took off his hat and said, "Morning,
Ma'am. I'm here to see Lawyer Lacey, if he's home."

The girl yawned and said, "His office is way over to
Main Street. I doubt he'll be home before six, if then. I
hope it's not important, sir. He said something at breakfast about being out of the office most of the day. You
might still catch him there, if you hurry, though."

Stringer stayed put as he smiled down at her and
said, "I fear I just might have. I came here when I noticed he didn't seem to be there. They call me Stringer
MacKail. I'm a newspaper man, working for the *San
Francisco Sun*. I was with your, ah, brother? when that
oil well blew up the other day. I see by the smoke that's
still rising above town that it's still burning. So I've

been trying to interview him about his plans to put it out."

She yawned again and said, "You'd best come into the parlor. I don't like to be seen in public like this. You say you want to write about us in the newspapers?"

He said he surely did. It still surprised him a mite to see how most folk reacted to the thought of seeing their names in print. As she led him from the door to the front parlor she said her maiden name was Victoria Lacey and began to spell it for him before he assured her he knew how to spell Victoria Lacey. She sat him on a davenport and joined him there as she began to pin up the red hair she'd let down for sleeping while explaining, "It's the last name people spell wrong, without the e. I can tell you as much as Jim may know about that blowout. The company's sending a team of experts to cap that well. They'd hardly expect a lawyer or even their regular drillers, here, to deal with such a mess. Jim told me it was all the fault of a foreman the company fired. They suspect he got the job with phony references."

Stringer got out his note book and went through the motions of taking down things he already knew in shorthand, as he tried not to admire her chest. It wasn't easy, thanks to the way her robe was hanging as she pinned hair with both elbows up like that. He said, "I heard they ran Twain out of Tulsa. I didn't know that was how come. Might you know who hired him in the first place, Ma'am?"

She sighed and said, "My brother, Jim, sort of. I mean he's sort of my brother and sort of hired that big fake when the old head driller quit and the head office asked Jim if he knew any top drillers here in Tulsa. It wasn't Jim's fault. That Twain gent came highly recommended by a wildcatter Jim had done some business with."

Stringer made a serious note in his pad as he asked, "Might we be talking about a wildcatter called Tex Roberts?" To which she answered, "Why, yes, now that you mention it. Do you know him?"

He said, "Not exactly. An Osage I know recommended him highly for sinking some oil wells on his spread. Might I ask how come you call Lawyer Lacey your sort of brother and gave Lacey as your maiden name, Miss Victoria?"

She dropped her hands listlessly to her lap, spoiling the view and looking rather sad for a Gibson Girl as she explained, "Jim is really my half-brother. We had different mommas and our daddy run off on both of 'em. So we grew up separate when his momma remarried rich and mine didn't."

He nodded understandingly and said, "I see you got back together at last," and she replied, "I guess we did. Jim looked me up six or seven months ago, back East, and said he'd just love to have me join him out here in the land of opportunity. I guess it was all right. He's been ever so kind to me."

He said, "Old Jim was a good sport about giving me a ride back to town the other day, too. You say you both started out named Lacey?"

She looked away as she murmured, "I still think of myself as Miss Victoria Lacey. Jim says it's just for now, until they get about to changing some silly laws. He says he can get me divorced with a few strokes of the pen and a wink at a judge he knows. But I still say I'll be switched with snakes before I'll ever let anyone call me Victoria Bluefeather! Isn't that about the dumbest name you've ever heard?"

Stringer tried not to smile as he told her, "Mayhaps they saw no need for you to use the name in polite society, either. It was just to get power of attorney for your half-brother as the in-law of Walter Bluefeather, right?"

She nodded and swung her big green eyes to meet his as she said, defiantly, "I swear to you I married that savage in name only! If that's what they even want to call it. I told Jim he was disgusting as well as crazy. But when he said I wouldn't even have to meet the man, let alone stand in front of an Indian minister with him, I had to give in."

She lowered her eyes to her helpless looking hands as she added, softly, "I had no place else to go. I broke up with the boy back East who'd been courting me when Jim wrote how rich we were going to get out here. I must have been crazy, too. But Jim treats me decent enough and I get to laze about and eat all I want. I suspect you don't believe I've never been in bed with any Indian in all my born days, right?"

Stringer said, gently, "I believe you. Walter Blue-feather told me he'd married a white gal in name only. Now that we've met, I feel sure he never could have seen you in the flesh."

She flustered the top of her robe back together as she blushed and said, "Oh, whatever could be wrong with me this morning? I swear I don't know why I'm sitting here half undressed, pouring my heart out to a total stranger like this! You must think I'm just a silly little fool!"

He shook his head soberly and said, "Nope. If I had to put a label to your sufferings, I'd call 'em cabin fever. You've got yourself stuck in a sort of gilded cage, even if it is painted mustard colored. You're too young

and healthy looking to lay slugabed with a box of choc-
olates and you dasn't try to make any friends in the
neighborhood lest they ask delicate questions you don't
want to answer. You just opened up to me, all at once,
because you found us sitting here like strangers on a
train and you've been just busting to talk about your
troubles with somebody who might not gossip to the
neighbors, right?"

She dimpled at him and said, "My, you *do* understand human nature of the distaff persuasion. I hope you
don't mean to print anything I just told you in your
paper!"

He chuckled and said, "Not hardly. I don't write a
gossip column and you have to be more famous to ap-
pear in the one we do run in the *Sun*. Nothing you've
told me is unlawful, exactly. Your Osage husband helps
run his tribal council and I doubt he lied to them about
your deal with him. Might you know if the BIA has you
down with an allotment number, you being a dependent
Indian family member and all?"

She looked incredulous and gasped, "Good heavens,
do I look like an Indian?" So he had to explain, "Lots of
folk with red hair and green eyes are listed as Indians by
the government. I know of a full-blooded Miwok barber
back in Calaveras County who never asked to be listed
at all. It's not what you look like that they worry about
in Washington. It's whether you want a fight with the
U.S. Army or a handout from the BIA that counts. The
famous Black Warrior of the Alabama Creeks was a runaway slave of pure African descent and they still had to
deal with him as a mighty wild Indian. Chief Ross of
the Cherokee never would have had to walk the Trail Of
Tears if he'd just moved into, say, Nashville and shut up
about it. Some of the soldiers marching him and his

people west likely had as much Indian blood, had they wanted to brag about it. I reckon I'll just see how they might have a Victoria Bluefeather listed with the BIA these days. I won't tell 'em I just met you or comment on your complexion, seeing as I hope we're friends."

As he reached for his hat and rose, she got to her own feet as well, asking, wistfully, "Must you go so soon? It seems you just got here and I've been so lonely!"

He gulped as she put her hands gently to his shirt front and added, "Can't you say just a little while longer? Jim won't be back for hours and I haven't had a chance to entertain you at all properly!"

He wondered how proper what she had in mind might be, and felt sort of wistful about that last time in old Irene's bathtub. If he was right about the smoke signals in this redhead's green eyes, he could still make a fool out of himself by grabbing her back, even if she really wanted him to.

But he felt sorry for the poor lonesome gal and it wasn't even noon, yet. So he said, "I reckon I could stay a mite longer if you're pining for company, Miss Victoria. But what do you want to talk about, now? I thought we just about covered all your depressing family secrets."

She said, "Let *me* be the judge of that," and took him by one hand to lead him out of her parlor. As they headed back along the hall toward what had to be her kitchen Stringer assumed he was in for some coffee and cake. She was muttering something about the boy back home she'd abandoned to go west and marry Indians. But when they got to the big kitchen she led him through it to what he expected to be an adjoining pantry. Only, when they got there, it turned out to be a bitty bedroom with an adjoining bath. She told him, "This would be the maid's quarters, if we had a live-in maid. We only have a Cherokee lady who comes in once a week."

Then she said, pointedly, "She's not due today and nobody else ever comes back here, if you take my meaning."

He did, but he still felt it best to warn her, "I don't know, Miss Victoria. I can tell you've been feeling neglected. But I'm just a tumbleweed kind of drifting through these parts." To which she replied with a knowing smile, "I'm glad. I can't afford to get involved this way with anyone from *Oklahoma*."

He didn't have to ask what she meant by involved, since she just shucked her robe to let it fall to the floor and stand there bare as Venus rising from the waves, saying, "Well. How do you like me so far?"

He liked what he saw a lot more than Irene back at the hotel might have wanted him to. Both of them had lovely bodies, but the contrast between this pale green-eyed redhead and the smouldering, tawny Irene was about as great as it could have gotten without one of them being ugly. So he shut the door behind him, made sure it was locked, and hung up his hat and gun rig to get his own duds off as Victoria threw herself down on the teal blue silk bedcovers, moaning, "Hurry! Hurry! It's been over a year!"

He believed the poor young gal as he lay down beside her to take her in his naked arms, hoping his fool pecker wouldn't let them both down after all the abuse it had suffered from a wild Comanche. But it didn't. For Victoria was mighty wild in her own right and just the thought of parting that carrot-colored love fuzz with it halfway up inspired it to rise to full attention before he'd done so, groaning, "Jee-zuss!" through clenched teeth as he felt what he was getting into. Going without sex as long as she had had swollen as well as lubricated her lips. But she wrapped her long white legs around him and hugged him deeper, moaning, "Oh, Lord, I'd forgotten how good this felt, even playing with myself so much!"

Then they were too busy kissing to talk about it for a spell. It seemed to drive her even wilder when he took longer than usual to climax, great as it felt. She took advantage of his hesitation to come thrice in a row before he pounded them both to full glory and went limp in her arms, gasping for breath and knowing he was done for if he took it out for some smoking and cuddling. Women never seemed to understand men, bless them, for she hugged him tightly with her thighs and crooned, "Oh, do you really want more? This is heavenly!"

Then she confided, with a teasing internal contraction, "I've never been ashamed of my warm nature. I just happen to be particular about who I do this with. You may as well know, now, that I did try to tell myself to behave, as we were talking out front and I saw you were staring at my little titties."

He laughed, kissed her, and said, "If they were all that little we might not be having this conversation. I was trying to behave myself, too. Ain't human weakness swell?"

She said, "I'm probably going to feel mighty ashamed of myself after you tumbleweed on. Meanwhile, I want to get on top."

He let her. He was no fool. And as she proceeded to do all the work, with him staring up at her bobbing

charms in broad daylight, he said, "You've got nothing
to feel ashamed of, pard. You're built swell enough to
pose for an art class, if only you were holding still."

She blushed and told him he was awful, even as she
leaned foreward to let him tease her nipples with his
tongue. If they hadn't been behaving so shamelessly in
bright light, he might not have been able to treat her so
right. But by the time it was his turn on top again he
was able to. It took her longer to come that time and as
they finally managed a long almost painful mutual climax, he felt the dumb thing quitting cold on him inside
her. She felt what was happening as well. But instead of
calling him a sissy she kissed him tenderly and murmured, "We'd better stop while we're sated for the moment. I must have been crazy to act like this under my
own brother's roof in broad daylight. But now that
we're sane again, at last. We really have to consider
possible consequences!"

He felt icy fingers up his spine but kept his own
voice calm and pleasant as he asked, "Oh? Don't you
know how to, ah, take care of yourself, honey?"

She kissed him again and said, "Good God, do you
think any girl would drag a total stranger into bed with
her if she didn't? I'm not worried about that. I just don't
know how I'd explain it if Jim came home unexpected!"

It would have been crude of Stringer to agree a
would-be loving relation might like it even less after
being turned down by a shy baby sister. So he agreed it
might be a smart move to quit while they were ahead
and she was back in her robe with her hair repinned,
looking as if butter wouldn't melt in her mouth, before
he could even get his boots on.

But as she walked him to the front door later, arm in

arm, she asked when they'd ever be able to do it some more. She said she could sneak out to his hotel. But he said, "That might not be a good idea. I'll get back in touch with you as soon as I come up with a safer place for us both."

CHAPTER
NINE

Some philosopher had once declared that no man was ever as sane as he was just after a really fine screwing. Stringer couldn't come up with the old gent's name but he felt sure the man must have screwed as well as thought a lot. Stringer knew the sanest course for him right now would be to check out of the Osage Inn, hop the first westbound at the depot, and write his feature on the way home from the notes he already had.

Sam Barca had only sent him here to do a Sunday page or two on the novel Oklahoma rock-oil boom. That oil well still burning in the old Creek graveyard offered plenty of local color and he had enough on the odd way oil well Indians were forced to do business to bore a crusty old editor with a nasty disposition and the fastest blue pencil in the west. It was no news that the oil business was a rough business, run by men who'd peddle their own mother's ass for an educated opinion on a good place to drill next. He knew old Sam Barca would chide him for taking it personal and there were paid lawmen here, red and white, to worry about who'd done what to whom and why. The smart thing for a newspaper man caught in the cross fire to do would be to just *git*, before he wound up another mystery for old Bill Tilghman to solve.

As he once more approached the Pronghorn on his way to the hotel, Stringer saw the white Buick wasn't parked there any more. It was likely just as well. He'd just taken a mighty dumb chance with Walter Bluefeather's legal spouse, without half her excuse for feeling hot and bothered, and did the big tough Osage ever find out, there was just no saying how he'd take to wearing horns, even in name only. Gals were as bad as men when it came to kissing and telling and Lawyer Lacey was sure to be steamed if he ever found out another man had messed with his baby sister. Now that he was sure he wouldn't want to even wink at a woman for at least a week, Stringer felt it was bad enough to have one set of enemies gunning for him for no good reason he could see. He didn't really need big brothers or husbands out to clean his plow. So, yep, it was just about time to get up from the table before the game got even rougher. Irene at the hotel was likely to be mighty upset by him checking out after promising her a late supper as well as a walk home. But she was likely to be even more upset by a man who couldn't get it up once he got her there, so what the hell.

Meanwhile, he'd missed his noonday dinner and old Victoria had never served him the coffee and cake a more proper hostess might have. He recalled the Pronghorn served a free lunch along with booze and ragtime music. So he turned in to see what they might have on the lunch tray down at the deep end of the bar.

The place was almost empty but the lunch tray was laden with hard-boiled eggs, pig's knuckles, salami, and potato salad. There would have been even more if Bull Durham hadn't been standing there stuffing his face, with a schooner of beer in his free hand and a Remington .44 hanging low on his hip. Bull's boots were made for riding as well. It wasn't easy to make out whether he considered himself oil or cow.

Stringer ordered a bottle of Steamer instead of draft, since he meant to eat more than he meant to drink, and bottled beer helped pay for the overhead. Then he carried it down to the free lunch to join Bull Durham, saying, "Great minds run in the same channel. Do you mind if I ask you a personal question, Bull?"

Durham shrugged and said, "Ask away. I got no secrets. The spud salad has gone a mite rancid, by the way."

Stringer bit into a boiled egg, washed it down with Steamer, and said, "I won't eat any, then. I've gotten just a mite curious about just what you do for a living, Bull."

Durham shot him a puzzled smile and asked, "What do you suspect I am, a Chinese laundryman?" So Stringer polished off the egg, reached for a slice of salami, and replied, "So far, I've never seen you do anything you could make much money at. I know you say you're an oil field man and I ain't about to call an armed man a liar. But we're in the middle of an oil field and this place'd be a lot more crowded if all those other roughnecks weren't out *working* in said oil field right now."

Bull Durham laughed, easily, and said, "Oh, I follows your drift. I could be taken for a bum, lazing about saloons day and night. But as a matter of fact, I'm on call twenty-four hours a day. It saves getting dressed and undressed if I stay up most the time."

Durham saw that had only raised Stringer's curious eyebrow higher. So he added, "I'm a licensed steam fitter and stationary engineer. I work for myself and they call me in, like, say, a locksmith, when there's trouble with the pipes or machinery. I get to wear cleaner overalls and riding boots because I sort of ride hither and yon, fixing things."

"What sort of things?" asked Stringer, and this time Durham wasn't smiling as he said, "I just told you. Oil field things. I fit pipes as need fitting, and who do you think they call when an engine breaks down? Most of the pumps can run untended with ball governors and automatic fuel and water feeds keeping an eye on things. A human eye has to check the gauges now and again. The regular crews worry about that. It's when the gauges read funny or the engines act odd that they send for me. Nine outten ten times I can fix it with a good bang from a wrench. The tenth time, I earn every penny I bill the big shots. You can't pump much oil with a broke-down engine or through a leaky pipe, you know."

Stringer ordered another Steamer to go with the oversalted free lunch before he said, "I stand corrected on your now more visible means of support, Bull. Seeing you get to traipse all over oil fields, though, might you be able to tell me where and how I'd be able to lay hands on, say, a chart showing all the wells and pipe lines going where?"

Bull Durham frowned dubiously and replied, "I wouldn't know where to begin. I know where I've strung pipes for clients. But I never saw fit to map 'em and, in all modesty, I ain't the only pipe fitter in the business. The notion is to just run as few lengths of oil line from the well to the refinery by the shortest route you can manage. That's often into a line already strung by the same producer. If there was such a map, the lines would look more like trees rooted at the refinery end and branching out ever which-ways than anything else."

Stringer asked, "Wouldn't each refinery have at least a chart of the pipes feeding into them? What's to stop a sneak from tapping the tree if nobody's keeping track?"

Bull Durham shook his head and said, "You don't carry oil to market in maple syrup buckets. The lines are *metered*, so any serious loss of oil would be noticed. That's how I get called in to fix leaks. As to private refinery charts, you'd play hell getting a look at one if there was one. Each company reads its own meters. They just don't *want* nobody else to know their production figures. I didn't see much sense in that, neither, 'til I was told production figures effects the price of oil stock way back East."

Stringer washed down another boiled egg and said, "Our financial editor might want me to pester the oil trust for such figures. I doubt my feature editor does. But as long as we're on the subject, have you ever done any work for a wildcatter they call Tex Roberts?"

Bull Durham hesitated, shrugged, and said, "I see no reason to fib when I don't have to. I supervised some pipe lines out to the Osage reserve a few months back and I still check some steam pumps for Tex out that way, say, twice a week. He bought good gear to begin with, so the pipe joints don't leak enough to care about and the pumps just about take care of themselves. I only have to tighten a bolt or adjust a gauge a notch now and again. What about old Tex?"

Stringer shrugged and said, "Just wondering. I was

out at the Rocking Tipi for ice cream, yesterday. Blue-feather seemed well satisfied with the services as well. But let's talk some more about oil meters. I didn't notice anything that impressive out yonder. Seemed to me the pumps just emptied into plain old pipe lines that ran together at the well closest to town."

Bull Durham nodded and said, "That's different. I ain't saying Indians steal slicker than the rest of us, but you are talking about a cluster of wells no white man's likely to look at more than once or twice a week. Blue-feather's private pipe line, or I should say Standard's line out to that cattle spread, gets metered at the *town* end before it joins the main trunk line to their local refinery. It's not that John D. don't *trust* noble savages, I feel sure, but a man with plenty of time and privacy has been known to jiggle a meter and that can add to many a barrel a day."

Stringer asked how one might go about changing the readings on an oil line meter and Durham asked if he wanted them numerical or alphabetical, adding, "The simple way it to just unscrew the face and move the numbers with the same screw driver. They do seal the meters with embossed lead seals but, like I said, a sneak with plenty of time and privacy can take a plaster cast of the original seal, bust it, and remelt the lead with a blow torch and stamp the same impression in it whilst it's still hot. Don't you never say I told you Walter Bluefeather would do a thing like that, though. He couldn't, even if he wanted to, the meters not being where he could get at 'em if he wanted to."

Stringer started to reach for another boiled egg, contented himself with downing the last of his second bottle, and told Bull Durham, "I never said I suspected an Indian stockman would be up to cheating John D.

Rockefeller in a business deal. But wouldn't having Bluefeather's production figures under total and secret control give Standard Oil an easy crack at cheating *him*?"

Bull Durham shook his head and said, "I'm going to tell you a trade secret. Old John D. is just as skinflint as they say he is. The story about him ordering three fried chickens for a dinner party, counting the drum sticks and raising hell when he only counted five is true. But Standard Oil don't cheat at figures. They can't afford to. They do too much business with too many folk to want word to get around that their word can't be trusted."

He finished the last of his larger schooner and put it on the bar as he continued, "Do you ever sign a contract with old John D., make sure you have a Philadelphia lawyer go over all the small print with you. For if there's one word about your dear old mother's blood on the paper, Standard Oil will take it if they have to fight you all the way to the Supreme Court. But if they say they mean to deliver such and such on such a date, you won't have to worry about it being the day after or the day before. Tex Roberts did Bluefeather a favor by signing his oil lease over to Standard. He figures to get every nickel he has coming to him until his wells run dry and, after that—tough shit."

Stringer sighed and said, "I've heard much the same about old John D., and that means another tedious trip to the BIA."

Durham asked, "What makes you so sure Bluefeather or any other Indian's getting cheated?" To which Stringer could only reply, "I don't. But somebody must be. For whoever's doing it tried to kill me and did kill an Indian agent. I somehow doubt that could mean they were cheating Chinamen. So it's been nice talking to you, Bull."

Stringer stepped back out into the dazzling sunlight alone as Bull Durham ordered another draft. Stringer thought once more of just going on back to his hotel and the hell with Tulsa as the noon day breezes blew hot dust and rock-oil fumes in his face. But somehow he found himself walking the wrong way, toward the BIA as he muttered to himself, "What do you expect to find there, save for paper cuts, you fool bulldog? They'll have it recorded that Walter Bluefeather has a white in-law acting as his sponsor or they won't. You already know he never could have sold his oil lease without a white man signing for him. Both Bluefeather and little Victoria told you Lawyer Lacey was that fool Indian's brother-in-law and there's no reason for both of them to fib to you about it. Do you really think Sam Barca cares if the BIA keeps good records or not?"

He swung a corner and started to cross the blazing dusty street to get to the meager shade on the other side. Then a shot rang out close behind him as someone yelled, "Stringer! Duck!" So he dove to the dust on his belly and lizard crawled on to the cover of a watering trough on the far side, fast.

But as he got rid of his hat and got out his gun to risk a cautious peek back the way he'd just come, he saw it was just about over. The blue-clad Jake Wetumpka was standing in the street with his own gun drawn, covering the dusky youth in a cow hand outfit at his feet. Stringer didn't see why. He could tell from where he crouched that the cuss the Indian Policeman had downed was dishrag dead and leaking blood or piss out both ends.

As he warily rose and put his hat back on, the Creek lawman called out to him, "He was throwing down on you from behind, MacKail. You got any notion how come?"

Stringer holstered his own six-gun as he strode out to join Wetumpka and his victim. He stared down soberly at the dead youth and said, "All I can say for sure is that he seems to have grown up Indian and dressed cowboy. I still owe you, Jake."

Wetumpka shrugged and said, "My pleasure. I get mighty tired of hearing how big and brave Osage are. This one was out to backshoot you like the coward he was born."

By this time they'd been joined by others, including the sadly smiling U.S. Deputy William Tilghman, who glanced down, shook his head wearily, and said, "I sure wish you hadn't done that, Jake. It's not that I doubt he had it coming, for we have papers on him as well. But this here Willy Whitepony was an Osage and there's already enough blood between his nation and your'n."

Wetumpka shook his head and said, "I don't reckon the Osage Council is apt to shed their tears or my blood over *this* no-good young son of a bitch, Bill. I had to gun him because he was about to gun Stringer, yonder. Before that he raped Miss Sageburner of the Osage Nation, and stole her daddy's horse while he was at it. He stole other things from his own people, too. Had the Osage lawmen caught up with him before I did they'd have gut-shot him and let him die slower. Any Indian who rats on his own people is considered lower than a shit-eating dog by his blood kin!"

Bill Tilghman allowed, "Well, the Starr gang was about as low as I can recall and they did raid Creeks and whites instead of Cherokee. So you may be right. I sure hope so, for your sake."

Then Tilghman turned to Stringer to ask, "How come

this outcast Osage was out to gun you, old son?"

Stringer said, "We were just talking about that. I never saw him before in my life. Someone must have hired him to do me in. Lord knows, he had no other sensible reason."

Tilghman sighed and said, "Life sure was less exciting around here before you blew into town, MacKail. You did say you was about ready to go back to Frisco, didn't you?"

Stringer nodded, but said, "Just give me another twenty-four hours, Bill. If I haven't figured it out by then I doubt I ever will."

Tilghman stared down at the body between them again as he considered, then said, "You're as likely to wind up in this unseemly condition as you are to find out what makes you so popular in Tulsa these days. But since I like you and you asked polite, you got until the noonday westbound tomorrow to solve your fool mystery, if you can, and be on that train whether you can or can't. Like the Indian Chief said, I have spoken."

Once they'd let him into the back offices at the BIA, Stringer told the branch chief, "I'm sorry to bother you again Mister Manson, but they will keep shooting at me and the back trailing seems to be taking me ever deeper into Indian country. Would you mind if I went over a few matters with the agent who mans your Osage desk?"

Manson sighed and replied, "I only wish you could. Agent Davis isn't with us any more. Pending his replacement his steno gal, Miss Tenkillers, would be the one for you to talk to. She handled all his paperwork, made telephone calls for him and such. Come on. I'll show you to her cubby-hole."

He did. Better yet, when he introduced Stringer to the pretty young lady, Manson ordered her to cooperate with Stringer in every way before he left them alone on either side of her small desk. She was blushing slightly, so Stringer figured she'd seen how Manson's words could be taken by a strange gent dressed in dusty denims and a speckled Stetson. There was no polite way to assure her he wasn't suffering a raging erection as they sized one another up. They said old Charles Dana Gibson used his own pretty wife as the model for the swell-looking gals he drew. He was tempted to tell this one that if anything ever happened to the original model she had a job just waiting for her, but he didn't. Somehow Gibson Girls didn't excite him as much as usual this afternoon. But noting the China blue eyes and elfin Irish features that went with her coal black shiny hair and olive complexion, he had to ask, "Might not Tenkillers be a sort of Cherokee name, Ma'am?"

She smiled wryly and replied, "It's nothing like *sort of*. My grandfather trod the Trail Of Tears and he said his feet still hurt until the day he died. Is there anything else you wanted to know about the Cherokee Nation, Mister MacKail?"

He leaned back in the leather-padded visitor's chair and told her, "Not hardly. I've already met some other Cherokee here in Tulsa and I'll take their word they're not after me. I'm more suspicious that someone was out to skin some Osage, or vice versa, and your boss was dealing with Osage matters the day he got murdered."

She listened intently and wise-eyed for such a pretty young she-male and by the time he'd brought her up to date on all his various close calls and suspicions, he'd gotten her to call him Stuart if he could call her Helen. She said it was all right if he smoked as well. But he liked her even better when she ducked out a minute to bring back the files on Bluefeather and some other Osage who'd had white folk sign contracts with the oil trust for them.

The dossier on Walter Bluefeather bore out everything Stringer had already learned. Miss Victoria was just mentioned as old Walter's lawful spouse, with a BIA number entitling her to rations and hunting ammunition if the family oil well ever ran dry. They didn't seem to care what color she'd started out. But Lawyer Lacey was recorded as a U.S. Citizen, meaning white, granted power of attorney by reason of family relationship.

Stringer asked, "Wouldn't it be just as fair and a lot less bother if you let an oil well Indian just hire the white rep of his own choice, Miss Helen?"

She shook her head and explained. "They used to allow that. No doubt you've heard of the notorious Indian Ring that ran hog-wild under the Grant Administration?"

He nodded but still looked puzzled. So she said, "From what I know of Walter Bluefeather, an Arabian rug merchant would have to get up mighty early to pull any wool over *that* Indian's eyes. But I fear that like every other race, we have dimwits and drunks among us. Add that to illiteracy, a poor grasp of English, and the money and land grants Uncle Sam showers on reasonably well behaved Indians, and it's a mighty tempting chicken coop for any fox, red or white. I could tell you tales of Indians being taken to the cleaners, even with all the regulations in place to keep that from happening."

He said, "Your boss already did. Walter Bluefeather doesn't seem to be having in-law trouble. But tell me what would happen to his oil money if he was to some-how wind up dead? Wouldn't his lawful spouse inherit his estate?"

Helen nodded grimly and said, "That was one of the things poor Mister Davis was talking about, just before he was killed in that dreadful saloon. He said he was going to talk to Bluefeather about entailing his estate to his oldest male blood relative of pure Osage descent."

Stringer whistled softly, asked if Davis might have done that before he was gunned, and when she said she didn't know, he put the Bluefeather papers aside to go through the others, observing, "I might just have an-other talk with Victoria Bluefeather nee Lacey. She asked me to, and we may not have covered everything she knows. Can't see her as a master crook. But then, if master crooks were easy to spot we'd call 'em *dumb* crooks."

He leafed through the other dossiers on oil well In-dians and failed to find Lacey listed as their white front. None of them seemed to be named Whitepony. When he mentioned that to the white Cherokee gal she said, "Heavens, I told you when you told me of that shoot-out that Willy Whitepony was no longer considered an Osage. Neither the Cherokee nor Creek would take him in as even a guest, after what he pulled on his own people. Would you take in a rascal who couldn't even be trusted by his own people?"

He said, "We do it all the time. General Santa Ana got to dwell in New York City after the Mexicans couldn't stand him any more. But maybe Washington isn't as sophisticated, or maybe it's too sophisticated about the smell of skunks."

He closed the last dossier neatly and began to roll the smoke she said he could as he continued, "If the late

Willy Whitepony was in bad with all three nations in this neck of the woods, he must have had some other reason for being in Indian country. How do you like him as a hired gun?"

She grimaced and replied, "I never liked him as a reservation Osage. He was obviously hired to murder you. He might have been the same one who murdered poor Mister Davis. Anyone can *say* they come from Texas and the witnesses who said anything at all said the killer was dressed cow hand."

Stringer sealed the smoke with his tongue and lit it before he decided, "That works. It was dark back there by the piano and so many cow hands in these parts look Indian, when one looks close, that nobody bothered to look close. Most of the old boys in the Pronghorn at the time don't seem to have looked at all."

He took a deep drag, let it out with a sigh, and said, "I sure thank you for your time and trouble, Miss Helen. But I still fear all I've found out for certain today, is that I'll be leaving town tomorrow, with or without all the answers. I'd rather try to get out of a contract with Standard Oil than a deal with old Bill Tilghman. So my time is running out, even as I sit here jawing about it, and I'd best get on down the road."

As he got to his feet she rose as well and asked him where he might be going next. He shrugged and replied, "If I knew I'd be proud to tell you. No matter which way I wander I seem to wind up moving in a circle. I might ride out to the Rocking Tipi again, and then I might just pick up my possibles and leave early. It's a hot stinky day for riding or even walking, and no matter where I ride or walk to I seem to get the same answers."

She sighed and said, "I wish there was more I could do for you." Then she brightened and added, "I know.

Why don't you meet me here after work and we can talk about it some more as you walk me home!"

He started to leap at the chance. Then he recalled what that philosopher had said about sanity and said, "I'll try. But don't hold me to it, Miss Helen. For I might get shot, or find something out, between now and . . . What time did you say this office closes for the day?"

She told him six P.M. and he repeated his warning not to bet the old homestead on it before he left, trying to tell himself not to be a total fool. Helen Tenkiller was so pretty it hurt. But he already had at least two Tulsa gals to worry about. Or might it be already three?

Finding his way back to where Pearl Starr was holed up was easy enough. Getting in to see her again was more complicated. Cousin Henry didn't seem to be there. But the white boy who'd disarmed him that first time told Stringer on the steps that Miss Pearl had already seen him and didn't want to be disturbed right now, since she was taking a bath.

Stringer said, "I can wait. I know my way to her sitting room, old son." But as he tried to step inside, the gunslick stiff-armed Stringer back against the railing and would have sent him ass-over-tea-kettle to the dust a full story down, if Stringer hadn't caught the rail.

Stringer didn't aim to go that way. So he bounced back off the rail and planted a fist in the tough's smart-ass smirk. The tough must have known more about gun fighting than fist fighting, from the way he landed flat on his back inside, bawling blue murder and groping for his gun. Stringer didn't want him to do that so he kicked the cuss in the balls as he drew his own gun and, while the resultant noise wasn't quite as loud as gunfire might have been, it was loud enough. So Pearl Starr came running in to join them, covered with soap bubbles and a towel that might have done more to hide her wet curves if it had been bigger.

As she took in the scene the young madam said, "Oh, it's you again. Have you gone mad with passion or is there something *else* I could do for you, MacKail?"

He said, "An Indian with a mean rep and a Colt '74 tried to shoot me in the back today. I was wondering, seeing you know so many vile-tempered Indians, what you might be able to tell me about that."

She said, "Let's talk about it inside. Cut that blubbering, Clem. Haven't you ever been kicked in the balls before?"

The man writhing on the floor groaned, "Not recent, and I've never enjoyed it. I'm going to get you, Stringer, as soon as I can get to my own feet again, hear?"

Stringer didn't answer as he followed Pearl Starr into that same sitting room. He wondered if she noticed that towel was only covering some of the front of her and that her bare back and all was turned to him as she said, "Pay no attention. Nobody gets nobody without my permit and I ain't made up my mind about you, yet."

She sat on the same davenport, patted it for him to sit beside her, and made a faint attempt to cover all her naughty parts with the damp towel until she saw she couldn't, let it fall to her lap, and stuck her bare chest out bold as brass to observe, "Oh, well, it ain't as if I have anything to hide. I'm sure you knew I had a nice pair to begin with, right?"

He grinned at her and said, "You've got a mighty handsome set to show off, Miss Pearl. But could we talk about my back, now?"

She shrugged her bare shoulders and said, "No Cher-

okee I know would gun anyone in Tulsa without my
say-so. I have enough on my plate. Cousin Henry had to
hop a freight this morning when he was told Bill Tilghman knew he was in town and didn't like it all that
much. I got the BIA pestering me about some of the
romantic marriages I arranged for oil well Indians, too.
So this'd hardly be the time I'd want to start another
feud. You told me last time that you wasn't out to cause
trouble for me and mine. I took you at your word. I'll
thank you to be good enough to take mine."

He said, "I just heard words to the effect that neither
Creek nor Cherokee thought much of a renegade Osage
who preyed on his own kind, Miss Pearl. But as long as
we're on the subject, might the Indian agent you were
having trouble with have been the late Mister Davis?"

She shrugged again and said, "Him, too. But it's that
prissy straw boss, Manson, who keeps threatening to
put us all in jail for defrauding the government. Do you
reckon that if my girls went to bed with their Indian
husbands, at least once, they'd be able to prove all them
marriages were fake?"

He laughed despite himself and said, "I doubt it
would upset the Indians and, no offense, your girls
could likely endure one more slice from a loaf that's
already been cut a mite. But getting back to Davis, and
taking you at your word, the fact he had reservations
about his wards marrying up with white sporting ladies
could hardly be the secret he was killed to keep from
telling anyone. He'd already told his boss and Manson
was alive and well when I spoke to him no more than an
hour ago."

The naked adventuress seated at his side said, "Well,
I don't have nothing to hide from you, as you can see."

Then, as she caught the amusement in his eyes she

added, "I mean secrets worth killing folk to hide. It's no secret I'm built swell and take after my dear momma when it comes to men. I meant that did I have something to hide from you, we wouldn't be having this flirtation. Cousin Henry would have gunned you long afore he had to hop that freight."

He smiled thinly and said, "Maybe. I don't seem to kill as easy as someone here in town must want."

She smiled back to say, "That proves my point. I could likely take old Clem out, myself. But when Cousin Henry goes after a man that man is as good as dead. Cousin Henry ain't no back-shooter. He beat a deputy marshal with a rep, just a spell back, and it was face to face in broad-ass day. You can look it up."

Stringer sighed and said, "I don't have to. President Teddy Roosevelt pardoned old Henry for the killing when the Cherokee Council convinced him their wayward youth would never be naughty again. Didn't he rob a bank a day after they let him out of jail that time?"

She grinned like a mean little kid and said, "He needed some traveling money, didn't he? He only promised not to shoot any more federal lawmen. I just told you he left town to save old Bill Tilghman's life, didn't I?"

Stringer chuckled and said, "It's all in how you look at such attempts at reformation, I reckon. I'm glad he's left town, too. Although it surely would have made a news story if your considerate cousin had decided to face Bill Tilghman fair and square."

He thanked her for easing his mind on so many matters and got up to leave. She rose as well, hardly bothering to hold the limp towel to her privates as she said, "I got to rinse this soap off, now. It's starting to itch. Would you like to come along and scrub my back?"

He said he surely would, if only he had the time, and he might have meant it if he'd awakened alone in bed that morning. For she was mighty pretty, even with clothes on, and about as clean at the moment as a gal like her could get.

She shot an arch look back at him as she wigwagged the other way and asked how much time he figured a mere man could last with the likes of her. Then they both laughed and she walked on back for her bath, striding hot, as if it was up to him to follow or die frustrated.

He left, feeling wistful about passing up a chance to go down in history as the lover of someone famous. But since his code didn't allow him to boast of his conquests, and since even a gent who did could hardly call Pearl Starr much of a conquest, it was likely just as well.

He didn't see old Clem on duty in the vestibule as he strode through. The reckless youth was doubtless enjoying some bed rest right now. That reminded Stringer that he felt as if he'd been dragged through the keyhole backwards, so he went next to his hotel for a long hot soak in a tub of his own and a short nap, if Irene would just stick to her switchboard long enough.

CHAPTER
TEN

The pretty little breed he'd had breakfast with looked
sleepy-eyed, herself, as Stringer started to pass the desk
with a wave and let it go at that, for now. But Irene
called him back to tell him, "That Mister Barca from
San Francisco has called you by long-distance, twice."

Stringer said, "That must have been thrilling. Did old
Sam say what was so important?" and she replied with a
studious frown, "He did, if I can remember it right. He
said to tell you that the police out yonder have just ar-
rested some big shot about bad things he was doing to
the drinking water and that you didn't have to worry
about the hired gun he'd sent after you because there
was only that one, called Holt, and you shot him instead. Where have you been all this time?"

Stringer sighed and said, "Getting shot at by someone the San Francisco Waterworks just couldn't have
had on the payroll. The shoot-out with Holt seems to

have made me famous here in Tulsa and I have been asking questions I'd never have thought to ask if I hadn't added one and one to get three. Did my boss have anything else to say, Honey?"

Irene shot a warning look at the room clerk reading a magazine in a comfortable lobby chair and told Stringer, "He said you was to come on home because he was only planning on so much copy, I think he said, and that you'd been here long enough to write a book. Does that mean you got to leave right now?"

He owed the sweet little thing common courtesy. So he tried to sound sort of heart-sick as he said, "Not this instant. But all good things come to an end, alas, and I sure hope I'll be man enough for proper goodbyes, later tonight."

She motioned him closer and leaned across the counter to tell him in a whisper, "I'm not sure I can make it tonight. I just got a Western Union wire from down home and it seems my fool kid brother is on his way here to seek his fortune in the rock-oil business. They didn't say when he'd be arriving. He might not get here for another day or more. But should he blow in on the train, tonight . . ."

"He might not understand." Stringer cut in, adding, "Mayhaps it's best if you just kiss me off at the depot. I'm still not sure when that ought to be. I still have a few last straws to grasp at before I leave, and I know I'm not leaving this side of a bath, forty winks and a decent meal."

She dimpled and whispered, "I can see you look bushed, but you did have a mighty nice scrub, you said, just this morning at my place, right?"

He said, dryly, "I've been sweating some, since.

We'll talk about it later, once I figure out what I'm talking about."

He dragged himself upstairs, almost fell asleep and drowned in the luxurious soak he treated himself to, and then he hauled a bitty brass alarm clock from his Gladstone and set it to wake him in four hours. They said Thomas Edison got by on only four hours sleep every day and old Tom was a hardworking cuss.

But it seemed Stringer had barely dozed off, bare-ass in his daylit bed, when the infernal alarm went off with a head-splitting clamor and, by the time he'd fumbled for it and hurled it against the far wall, he was awake enough to swing his bare feet to the floor and curse them until he woke up entire. He'd bought such an indestructable alarm clock with such procedure in mind. So as he got up and tottered after it to make it stop ringing, he wiped the last sleep-gum from his eyes and promised his growling stomach he'd sate it as soon as he got dressed, damn it.

By the time he'd polished off a second cup of coffee in the cafe down the street, it was just after six and that nice little Helen Tenkiller would be leaving for home without him if he didn't run like hell for the BIA.

He ordered another coffee instead. A man who thought with his glands instead of his brains could make a fool of himself, even when his glands were more wide awake.

By the time he left the cafe he had his head awake, at least, and he felt more spring in his step than there'd been when he'd strode away from Pearl Starr's kind offer.

He thought about her some more as he trudged over toward the sprawling Tulsa railroad yards. Pearl Starr was no prettier but a lot more sinister than any other

ladies he'd met in these parts. Yet, taking her story with
a grain of salt, she had had him in her power and hadn't
even screwed him, and she openly admitted she was in
the business of getting around BIA regulations for fun
and profit. So he failed to see what else a gal who covered her bare behind so casually might have to hide.

In the glory days of the late Sam and Belle Starr the
gang had never been distinguished for subtle moves.
Old Sam had been a not-too-bright thief and old Belle
had sheltered thieves and fenced their loot for more fun
than profit. Henry Starr and his white kissing cousin,
whether they kissed all that much or not, were if anything', less cautious than their late uncle. As Pearl had
pointed out, the current muscle of the clan had a rep for
just going after anything or anybody he wanted. Hiring
someone else to do such chores was hardly Henry's
way.

That left red-headed Victoria and the lighter and
darker breed gals, Helen and Irene, to go over again for
nits. But he saw no reason to strain his brain any more
about she-male suspects when there so many rough men
in town. One of 'em was a railroad yard bull who
popped out from between two tank cars to ask Stringer
who he was and where he thought he was going.

Stringer flashed his press pass at the semiliterate and
added he was looking for the Standard Oil refinery. The
yard bull waved his club at a tall skinny pipe flaring
smoky red flame into the darkening sky to the east as he
said, "They're just under yonder burn off if you want to
try. I doubt they'll let you in at this hour, though. The
office is likely closed for the night and I doubt the lob-
ster shift will let you through the gate."

Stringer thanked the yard bull and moved on. As he
swung around the end of a train of greasy tank cars he

could see why they called those bigger things rising above a cluster of frame shacks cheesebox stills. That was what they looked like, albeit made of riveted boiler plate and somewhat larger. He didn't try to figure the birdcage of piping, fat and skinny, that rose around the dark massive stills. He knew that, this far from the eastern markets, crude rock-oil was refined in batches, piped into tank cars, and shipped out as kerosene, gasoline, motor oil and whatever. There was a lot of wastage to be burned off or dumped in the nearby Arkansas. A lot of the separates had little or no market until someone figured out some uses for petroleum jelly and wax, let alone the black tar they wound up with in the end.

As he approached, he saw that the only fence around the layout was three-strand barbed wire. So he cut some of the distance by just ducking through the west corner of the property and ambling on toward the office sheds through the confusion of pipes laid across or above the cindery bare dirt.

As he passed under one elbow he heard soft hissing and sniffed mighty rotten eggs. He knew enough chemistry to be just as glad he wasn't smoking at the moment. Hydrogen sulphide was inflammable in its own right and the odorless methane that made up most of natural gas was downright explosive. It was a hell of a way to run an oil refinery.

He said so when he strode into the office shed to find a pair of gents hovering over blueprints on a center chart table. One wore a denim work shirt, and the other was in vest and white shirt sleeves. He was the one who growled, "We know about that leak. We've sent for a trouble-shooter. Was there anything else you wanted to tell us, cowboy?"

Stringer got out his press pass again as he told them

who he was, and said he wanted some information they might have. The one who seemed to be a plant manager stuck here past his usual supper time said, flatly, "This is not the Tulsa Public Library. You are trespassing on the property of Mister John D. Rockefeller and we're not authorized to gossip about his business. We're pretty busy at the moment, too, so why don't you go play someplace else, kid?"

Stringer smiled thinly and said, "I reckon I could just wire my paper that one oil well is burning out of control here and that Standard Oil has no comment on any explosions that are likely to take place any minute."

The plant manager straightened up to look more friendly as he hastily assured Stringer, "Hell, we're not facing any real emergency, here, Mister, ah, MacKail. It's just a stubborn gas leak our own crew can't seem to stop entirely. I'll allow you may hear a big whump if she ignites before the gent we sent for gets here. But we're not talking about a disaster to the plant, itself. We're just not leaking that much gas."

Stringer said, "I can still tell you where it is, if you don't know. There's this big elbow in a mighty fat pipe, with a big two fisted valve on top of it and . . ."

"We know where it is. It's the valve packing that's leaking," the plant manager cut in, glancing at the wall telephone across the room as he muttered, "That damned Durham should have gotten here by now."

Nobody seemed interested in throwing him out, after all, so Stringer stepped closer to the table to ask, "Might we be talking about a pipe fitter called Bull Durham, hangs out in the Pronghorn Saloon a lot?"

The blue collar refinery man was the one who said, "That's him. He has office space with a lawyer just above the Pronghorn. The secretary I just talked to said she thought he was downstairs and that she'd have him come right over. I wonder what could be keeping him."

Stringer asked if they were talking about a telephone in the office of Lawyer Lacey and when he was told they were he sighed and said, "Durham might have spotted me as I was cutting cross the yards ahead of him."

The plant manager frowned at Stringer to demand, "What reason might Bull Durham have for avoiding your company, MacKail?" So Stringer said, "I'm still working on that. I take it you do business with a client of Lawyer Lacey, Walter Bluefeather?"

They both looked blank. The plant manager said, "Hell, we refine oil for lots of oil well Indians with funny names. How am I supposed to know?"

Stringer said, "You could look it up. I know you wouldn't have oil leases or other such documents on file here at the business end of the oil game, but you would have charts on your own oil lines, wouldn't you?"

The plant manager nodded cautiously but asked, "Just what are you sniffing around for, MacKail?" So Stringer explained, "I don't suspect Standard Oil of anything but capitalism. But someone else here in Tulsa has sure been acting shy about their own sneaky doings. I'd be able to tell you better what it was, if you'd let me have a look-see at your pipeline blueprints. You have my word I'm not out to make your outfit look bad, unless Standard Oil is *in* on it, of course."

The two Standard Oil men exchanged thoughtful glances. The one in greasy denims shrugged and said, "Don't ask me. I just work here." So the plant manager pondered on a while and then he decided, "We have nothing to hide. I doubt we have anything that can do you any good, either."

He stepped over to a cabinet of flat blueprint drawers and asked which section of the Tulsa field they might be talking about. When Stringer allowed he was interested in the trunk line running beside the Pawhuska Post Road on the Osage reserve, the oil man said that was easy and hauled out a big blueprint covered with little white dots and skinny lines.

He laid it flat on the table for Stringer's inspection. The first thing Stringer noticed was that oil wells were only indicated by numbers with no mention of who might own what. When he said so the plant manager explained, "We're not concerned here about which infernal Indian's sponsor gets the royalty check from the main office. We just meter each line and credit the production to its number. The company paper pushers know which oil lease goes with which number. I told you this chart wouldn't tell an outsider all that much. It's not supposed to."

Stringer didn't answer as he ran a finger along the trunk line from town to the cluster of dots that had to be the wells he'd seen on Bluefeather's property. He got out his notebook to take down the number. Then, while he was at it, he made notes on oil wells further out on the Osage reserve. There were more of them than he'd expected. He chuckled and said, "This is one time the Indians would seem to have won." Then he traced some other white spiderweb lines in the direction of the refinery, nodded, and put away his notes, saying, "I told you I didn't suspect Standard Oil. But some local boys may want to explain some of the figures I just took down and, seeing it's almost sundown, I'd best get cracking. I wouldn't want to call on anyone, along with some law men I know, after bedtime."

They both naturally asked what he knew about Indian

oil leases that they didn't. So he shook his head wearily and just said, "You boys here at the refinery couldn't know as much as I did when I got here. Your job is to refine and ship the final product. The crude is what they've been crooking, long before you do a thing to it, and it's sort of complicated. So I'll just send you free copies of my paper, once I get it figured out a mite better, myself."

He left and headed back the way he'd come in the gathering dusk. As he approached the big elbow of pipe that smelled so bad he saw someone was standing there, as if it was some kind of gate. Stringer kept on walking, feeling tenser, until he could see it was Walter Bluefeather, his own gun already out, though held politely down beside him. Stringer nodded gravely and said, "Evening, Walter. I guess Bull Durham told you where I might be found at this hour, right?"

The big Indian nodded his big white hat and replied, "He sure did. And I'm sorry as hell about this. For I've kind of got to like you, MacKail."

Stringer answered, "I sort of like you, too, Walter. You're about the smartest Indian I've ever met. Of course, I can't speak for the other members of your Osage Council, once they find out just how slick a businessman you've really been all this time. I suppose you promised Willy Whitepony you could get him back into the good graces of his nation if he'd do just one small favor for you?"

Bluefeather grimaced and said, "That's what comes of sending a boy to do a man's job. Seeing you got to Standard Oil after all, despite my best efforts, just what might they have told you, and vice versa, just now?"

Stringer had to think about that. For, while telling the two-faced Bluefeather the jig was up might inspire him to just light out in his new Buick for parts unknown, those two men in the office were unarmed and not expecting any sudden Indian attacks.

As Stringer pondered his best choice of words, Bluefeather said, "I know you're stalling in hopes it might be darker when you crab for cover ahint them other pipes. I hope you can see I could have nailed you afore you spotted me, here, if I wasn't such a conversational cuss. So converse at me, Stringer. I'd like to know just how much you found out with your nose in the private matters of the Osage Nation."

Stringer shrugged and said, "It was only a suspicion before you proved it by this tense discussion we're having. I doubt the other Osage will be sore at me for taking a closer look at the way you've been protecting their interests as a council member and ice cream manufacturer, Walter. I doubt throwing down at me with that fine .45 would do you all that much good at this late date, either. If I were you I'd crank up that gas buggy you just bought and head for somewheres like, say, Tibet. Your fellow Osage are mighty fine trackers and they have a lot more than me to be pissed about."

Bluefeather shook his head and said, "Not if they never find out. So long, Stringer, I'll really miss you."

Then he swung the .45 up to fire as Stringer dove sideways shouting, "Don't do her, you damned fool!"

Then Stringer was flat in the dirt behind a massive length of iron pipe and Bluefeather had fired from within the cloud of natural gas he'd been standing in.

The "Whuff" the plant manager had said it might be sounded more like a cannon going off close to Stringer, as the refinery yards lit up red white and blue, and grainy gunk rained down from the ruby sky on Stringer and the pipe he lay huddled behind. As the light began to fade away, he saw Bluefeather's big hat a few yards away, charred black and still smouldering. So he raised a cautious head, his own gun drawn, and muttered, "Oh, shit, I *told* you not to do that!" as he spied what was left of the Osage under the elbow, where a roaring flame still played from the ruptured valve above.

As he eased in for a better look by the flickering light, he was sorry he had to. There was no smell of rotten eggs in the air, now. It smelled more like a ham that had been left in the oven to overbake. Bluefeather's body lay naked save for charred boots and gun belt, but his flesh was charred so matchhead crisp that he didn't look immodest. His privates had burned down to smouldering embers. His face looked even worse. The blackened remains of the face had been stretched into a ghastly grin by the heat of Bluefeather's partial cremation.

Stringer heard running footsteps and turned, gun in hand, as the two oil men from the office and another who'd been on duty somewhere else tore his way, all three with fire extinguishers in their hands. Stringer said, "I'd just let that valve go on burning for now, if I was you. You just heard what happens when you strike a light around gas that's *not* burning."

The plant manager saw what was still smouldering under the flaming valve and gagged, "What on earth have you been up to here?" To which Stringer could only reply, modestly, "Cooking with gas. Now, if you boys will be good enough to take over, here, I have some other pressing chores to tend to."

CHAPTER
ELEVEN

Later that evening, a drunk stepped into an alley near
the depot to take a leak and wound up pissing on his
own boots when Bull Durham rose ominously from behind his fort of ash cans to growl, "It's good to see you,
Pecos. I've been feeling sort of confused, tonight.
What's been going on out yonder?"

The drunk stared owl-eyed until the faint light from
the red skies above let him in on who he might be talking to. Then he said, "You're in deep shit, Bull. They
got the fried mortal remains of Walter Bluefeather in
escrow at the Tulsa Morgue because the Osage say it
would take the U.S. Cavalry and Artillery combined to
bury him on Osager ground. The Creek don't want him,
neither. The federal lawmen are hunting *you* now, with
the Indian Police helping. It's the first time I can recall
Cherokee, Creek and Osage agreeing what time of day
it is. But they surely seem agreed on the pain of being

screwed out of oil money. How much did you screw 'em out of, Bull?"

Durham stepped around the ash cans to converse more intimately with good old Pecos as he replied, "I wasn't the mastermind as set it up. I just done what I was paid to do and there wasn't supposed to be no trouble."

He glanced toward the alley entrance and added, "There would not have, if some other idjets hadn't stirred up that nosy young newspaper man and got him peeking under the walnut shells faster than we could shift the pea."

Pecos buttoned his pants and opined, "That MacKail kid sure must be smart. You and old Bluefeather even had Bill Tilghman fooled and here MacKail went and caught you at it less than a week after getting here a virgin."

Then he blinked at Bull Durham and added, "What did he catch you boys at, by the way? Nobody I drink with seems to know just what you was all up to, 'cept it being mighty serious, seeing how you have so many lawmen after you."

Durham said, "Never mind the whys of it, old pard. Tell me the *hows* of what they're up to. I know they have the livery covered. I damn near walked into a trap when I studied on my favorite mount and some moonlight riding down the old owlhoot trail. What about the railroad yards?"

Pecos sounded almost cheerful as he replied, "Oh, they'll nail you certain, if you try to hop a train out, Bull. Chris Madsen is set up in the depot, with some young gals serving coffee and cake as the boys finish a sweep of the yards and rest up to go sweep it some more. The Indian Police are set up all around the city limits, mounted up and spoiling for a horse race. I don't see how you're going to get away, Bull."

Bull Durham shrugged and said, "A man's got to try. It's been nice talking to you, Pecos. I hope you can see why I can't afford you talking to anybody else. It's nothing personal."

The old drunk began to sober up, sudden, as he stared wide-eyed down at the gun on Durham's hip and pleaded, "Aw, I wish you wouldn't kill me, Bull."

But Durham did. Not with the gun Pecos was staring so hard at but with the bowie the old drunk never saw coming until it had ripped into his belly and severed his aorta. It was barely possible for a man bleeding to death like that to let out at least one good yell. So, as Pecos dropped to his knees at Durham's feet, clutching his ripped-open belly with both blood-slicked dirty hands, Durham cut his throat from ear to ear.

The killer knew enough to crawfish backwards as he did so. So while he got some blood on his pants below the knees it hardly showed amid all the oil spots.

Durham knew he was in enough trouble without having to explain lurking in dark alleys with dead folk. So he slid out and slithered on, moving from shadow to inky shadow cast by the red glow above. He knew there was one way out of town the law might not have thought of. It hadn't occurred to him until he'd hunkered in that alley, sweating ants a spell.

Old Bluefeather hadn't motored back out to the Rocking Tipi this evening, thanks to that dumb response to Stringer MacKail's poking about the Standard refinery. So that speedy Buick runabout was still in Tulsa, someplace, and there wasn't an Indian pony made that could outrun a horseless carriage across open range.

Walter had usually parked it out front of Lawyer

Lacey's office. Durham also knew where the two-faced Osage parked when he didn't want just everyone to know he was in town. So that was where Durham made for, sliding between buildings and jumping a backyard fence or two until he was surrounded more by private residences. Some few folk were still seated on their front porches as Bull Durham passed, trying to walk innocent, but most had already called it a day. The fugitive felt a pang of envy as he passed a window where a gal was letting down her hair on the far side of her lace window curtains. He knew that even if he made it, he faced some lonesome time under the cold uncaring stars of midnight. They'd be expecting him to streak for Kansas to the north or Texas to the south, since either direction offered quick ways out of Oklahoma Territory, with Texas being the safest destination, though a longer trip to make on only one tankful of gasoline. He meant to streak for Fort Smith instead. There was a gal there he knew who let her hair down pretty good at night, or by broad day if a man asked her nice. But to get to her he had to get to old Walter's horseless carriage and, if that fool Indian had left it somewhere else . . .

But good old Walter hadn't, Durham saw, as he moved down yet another alley to spy the white paint job winking at him faintly from the ruddy gloom. Durham drew his six-gun and eased closer, eyes peeled and ears so wide open he could hear his own heart beats and a cricket chirping a city block away. As he got to within pistol range of the silent gas buggy. Durham took shelter behind a telephone pole and called out, softly, "I see you, there, you sneaky rascal! Come out with your hands up or I'll blow your infernal head off!"

There was no answer. Durham hadn't expected any, but a man just couldn't be too careful at times like these. He moved in the rest of the way and murmured, "Howdy, Miss Buick. You and me are going to take a little spin down the owlhoot trail at twenty or more miles an hour, Lord willing, and I sure hope Walter gassed you up right."

He holstered his gun and slid into the driver's seat to strike a match and read the dashboard gauges. He shook out the match with a grin when he'd read he had close to ten gallons to go on. Old Walter had bragged on getting twenty or more miles to the gallon and Fort Smith was only about a hundred and sixty-odd miles away.

Bull Durham had never driven this particular make, but all automobiles seemed to work much the same. He set the choke lever and made sure the brakes were locked. The gas pedal one used on the road was useless until you got the motor turning over, so there was a hand throttle to take care of that. He made sure the gears were in neutral. Then he climbed out and walked around to bend over and give the hand crank a good twist.

Nothing happened. Not even a cough from the infernal, and no doubt, cold engine. Bull Durham tried again, putting his back into it, this time, and still the muley son of a bitch refused to even backfire.

Durham swore, rubbed his sweaty palms dry on his pants, and got set to try again. Then Stringer told him, in a conversational tone from his stakeout in the shadows across the way, "It's no use, Bull. I disconnected the magneto wires a time back, and I sure hope you see the advantages of putting both your hands flat on the hood, right now."

Bull Durham must not have. He dropped to one knee and drew his own gun as he spun to face Stringer. Stringer fired and blew the crooked pipe fitter's brains out the back of his skull.

As the body lay limp as a stomped snake in the dust, with one foot twitching a mite, Stringer stepped out of the shadows, muttering, "Aw, you shouldn't have done that, you asshole. I wanted to *talk* to you about your crooked ways."

Bull Durham didn't answer. His one boot had even stopped twitching as Stringer hunkered over him to strike a match and mutter, "Damn, I fired higher than I aimed. It sure is tough to get the details out of gents like you and old Walter, thanks to your hasty habits."

Then he shook out the match and got up to stand to one side as he heard windows and doors popping open up and down the alley. Someone came to a backyard fence to see what they could in the flickering, uncertain light, and a she-male voice demanded to know what was going on. Stringer called back, "It's over for now, Ma'am. The law probably heard it too, and ought to be here any time, now."

The inquisitive woman called back, "Is that you, Stuart?" and so he replied, "It sure is, Miss Helen Tenkiller? I thought I recognized your voice, too. You live around here?"

She laughed uncertainly and said, "Why, no, I was only out strolling in the dark, without an escort. I thought you were going to escort me home after work, Stuart."

He said, "Something else came up. Don't come no closer. I just put one of them crooks we were talking about down, here. I was hoping to get more out of him when I spotted Walter Bluefeather's horseless carriage in this alley and suspected that as he had no further use for it, someone else might."

He only got to explain a little more when they were joined in force by Deputy U.S. Marshal Tilghman and a modest posse of lesser lawmen. When Tilghman demanded an explanation for the discharge of firearms within the city limits, Stringer identified himself and added, "Hold on. I'll shed more light on the subject."

Bill Tilghman and his boys were made of sterner stuff, but little Helen gasped and said, "Oh, how dreadful!" once Stringer had the Buick's brass headlamps gleaming on Bull Durham's body and scattered brains. Tilghman nodded and said, "Good thinking, Stringer. That would be Bluefeather's gas buggy, right?"

Stringer nodded and holstered his reloaded .38 as he replied, "Old Bull must have been planning on going somewhere sudden. When I noticed it wasn't parked near the Pronghorn as usual, I started looking for it. I didn't see how Bluefeather could have driven home this evening. I tried to take Durham alive. As you can see, I failed. He must have had more on his conscience than I figured. He couldn't have been the mastermind behind all this disgusting business."

Tilghman sighed and said, "Dang it, Stringer, I still don't have a clear picture of what's been going on, let alone who's been masterminding it. You lit out on us again right after you said Walter Bluefeather had taken advantage of his position on the tribal council to crook other oil well Indians. I don't want to wait until I read about it in your infernal *Frisco Sun*. I'd like a full explanation here and now!"

Stringer nodded soberly and said, "Here and now is sort of grim and there's some chill in the air as well as no place to sit down." Then he turned to the pretty part-Cherokee peering over the fence at them and added, "Do you reckon we could talk things over in your kitchen, Miss Helen, seeing you're still fully dressed and might be interested as well, working for the BIA and all?"

She allowed she'd even be proud to coffee and cake them. So Bill Tilghman told his junior lawmen to mind Durham's remains until the meat wagon arrived and to impound the horseless carriage while they were at it. Then Helen opened her back gate and led Stringer and Tilghman across her yard and up her kitchen steps.

Tilghman said she had a nice place here as he and Stringer took off their hats and sat down at the kitchen table. Helen thanked him and lit her fancy new gas range to make coffee before she joined them at table, saying, "It should be ready in just a few minutes. Now, what was that about my office being interested in those awful men, Stuart. I'm all ears."

Stringer smiled at her and said, "The rest of you ain't bad, neither. Beginning at the beginning, we all know oil was struck here and, even burning away most of it, there's still enough gas to cook with local. So Tulsa has been growing by leaps and bounds with almost everyone getting prosperous, too fast to keep track of. It might have been simpler if your BIA didn't have so many complicated regulations about Indians that suddenly had so much oil to sell, no offense, but that's the way things turned out, with hardly anyone having a grasp of the whole picture. The oil trust was playing with its cards close to its vest. The wildcatters have always been even more secretive. So as wells and pipe lines got all tangled up, the real brains behind Bluefeather, Durham and others saw the chance to skim some cream. Nobody else was likely to notice, since everyone was getting more milk than they'd ever expected."

Tilghman said, "Back up, Stringer. Right after you

blowed up Bluefeather you told us he'd been crooking the other Osage with sneaky pipe lines."

Stringer nodded and said, "It was Durham, out back, who laid the lines as a licensed pipe fitter nobody saw fit to question. He subcontracted to the wildcatter, Tex Roberts, who'd drilled on the Osage reserve and just wanted to get paid off and git. He might or might not have seen Durham and his pickup crew of ignorant hands put in the main trunk lines before Standard Oil bought the whole field out. All the oil trust had to worry about was the oil flowing in for them to refine and ship. They didn't pay for any oil they never run through a meter. If they noticed their blue prints of Durham's layout seemed a mite more spiderwebby than they might have done it, they had no reason to care. They hadn't done it. They didn't care how much pipe a small-time handy man used to get the results a less confused engineer might have. Do you mind if I smoke, Miss Helen? My mouth is sort of dry from all this talking."

She told him to go ahead and the coffee was almost ready as Bill Tilghman swore under his breath and said, "Get to the infernal *point*. How were Durham and that Indian swindling the other Osage?"

Stringer got out the makings and proceeded to build himself a smoke at the table as he explained, "Oh, that was easy, once I noticed how some wells leased by more honest Osage seemed to have more than one pipe line connected to 'em. Like I said, it looked sort of like a big old spiderweb. With some skinny white lines connecting crossways to the main trunk running in from old Walter's wells. To any Osage riding after cows out there, the needless pipes running who-knows-where would have looked like some other white man's notion. Few cow hands, red or white, care about pipe lines,

telephone poles and such, as long as they don't seem to
be in his way. Anyone who did have questions could
just ask the tribal council and, being good old Walter
was the member who served swell ice cream and knew
all about dealing with the oil trust . . ."

Tilghman whistled and said, "Pretty slick. They let
all the other oil well Indians get regular payments for at
least some of the crude under their own property while
Bluefeather's metered trunk line delivered the lion's
share! It's no wonder he could afford to discard Stanley
Steamers like smoked-down cigar butts! Yet, all the
time, the neighbors he was robbing were getting enough
to be pleased, even if he hadn't been the one trusted
tribal official they'd naturally turn to if they suspected
one penny of their oil money was lost strayed or stolen!"

Helen got up to fetch the coffee and cake as she
gushed, "That must have been what poor Mister Davis
had caught on to, just before they killed him, right?"

Stringer sealed his smoke and lit it before he told her
and Tilghman, "Not hardly. Davis was an Indian agent,
not an oil field expert. I'd say he was looking into the
way so many Indians were suddenly sprouting white in-
laws for sponsors. Had they let him live, he might not
have uncovered anything everyone else in the territory
didn't know. The Oklahoma Indian tribes seem to be as
able to take care of themselves in a business deal as,
say, your average immigrant homesteader. But his
snooping must have made the mastermind nervous.
Folks with guilty consciences tend to strike like snakes
instead of waiting to find out if they've been caught."

He took a thoughtful drag on his neatly rolled cigarette and added, "It's a funny thing. Right not I'd be
filing a report on that big fire just outside of town, or

even on my way home, if said mastermind had just kept cool. I was never sent here to pester Standard Oil about blue prints. I doubt poor old Davis could have gotten them to show any to him. So I'd say his murder was dumb as well as dirty."

Bill Tilghman growled, "Sinclair Oil has that run-away well on the run with the wagon loads of wet mud they've been hauling out of the Arkansas all day. The dumb brute who done that deed is in jail right now. Who do I get to arrest as the mastermind of that more serious matter? Lawyer Lacey, the one as set things up so's Bluefeather could peddle his and everyone else's Indian oil?"

Stringer didn't answer as Helen Tenkiller placed empty cups and saucers in front of the two of them. As she moved away from the table again Stringer shook his head and said, "Jim Lacey is just a lawyer, making him as dirty dealing a rascal as any other lawyer, but I'd say he was too dumb as well as dirty to have come up with such a tricky plan. Lacey's just a small town lawyer willing to marry his sister off just to make a buck, and while *she's* mighty sneaky about *some* things, she failed to strike me as all that smart. She just got out here from the east and can't know much about the cow business, let alone the oil business. Once Bluefeather had been recruited to go along with a slick scheme, I can't see him ever coming up with on his own, either, he had to have a white sponsor to peddle his own and other Indian's oil. He might well have married Victoria Lacey in name only, fair and square, before he was approached by the real slicker. You can look all that up, later. I doubt it will ever matter, now that Lacey has lost a client and his sister is a widow."

Helen placed a generous slab of fudge cake before

each of them and began to pour their coffee as she asked, with a puzzled frown, "Won't being Walter Bluefeather's widow put this horrid white woman in line for all that oil money, Stuart?"

Stringer smiled across the table to ask Tilghman, "Do you want to tell her, Bill?" So the older lawman explained, rather pompously, "Not hardly, little lady. Nobody gets to inherit ill-gotten gains, even when the Osage Nation isn't mighty interested in 'em. If the Laceys have a lick of sense, they won't try to put in for a nickel of Indian money. Ain't you fixing to join us, Ma'am?"

Helen shook her head and sat down again, saying, "I just ate, and even if I hadn't all this excitement has my tummy full of butterflies."

Then she turned back to Stringer to ask, "Who do you think could be behind all this excitement, Stuart?"

Stringer shot a warning look at Tilghman, who'd just picked up his coffee cup, and said, "I wouldn't drink that if I were you, Bill. I know it sounds mighty wild, but she did have her boss murdered for less reason, you know."

There was a moment of silence you could cut with a knife, then Tilghman slowly put his cup down, untasted, and said softly, "I sure hope you know what you're talking about, old son," and, before Stringer could reply, Helen Tenkiller sobbed, "You must be crazy, drunk, or both!" as she started to rise from the table.

Bill Tilghman said, quietly, "Sit down and stay set, Ma'am. I mean that, even if he sounds sort of loco to me, too." Then he nodded at Stringer and said, "Go on, seeing you made that dreadful accusation about a mighty pretty lady, old son."

Stringer sighed and said, "I think she's pretty, too. She asked me to walk her home this evening and I might have, if I hadn't been such a sissy. Her swell invite was no doubt issued with a colder welcome here than coffee and cake. She had a heap of time after I left her office to get in touch with her old pal Walter and have him waiting for us here. I'd say that was how come his new gas buggy was parked out back."

They were both staring at him in flabbergasted silence, so he blew smoke out both nostrils like an impatient old bull and told Tilghman, "Add it up, Bill. She was working in the BIA office, with files at hand just crammed with information about everybody. Her boss, Davis, was in charge of the Osage desk. Yet, when I stopped by to talk of such matters this afternoon she showed me useless files on Creek and Cherokee. She allowed, sort of casual, she knew who Walter Bluefeather might be. She had to, being he was the most important Osage they had files on."

He smiled at the pale faced part-Cherokee to add, "You let me take a peek at a handful of other Osage married up to get into the oil business. You figured it'd look suspicious if you didn't have *anything* on Osage at the Osage desk. But I can count, and even just counting numbers, I saw the moment I looked at that oil field blueprint that there were ten times as many Osage in the rock-oil trade than you ever allowed there was."

She started to cry. Bill Tilghman stared hard at Stringer to say, "Aw, now look what you've gone and done. I find that gas buggy parked out back a mite sinister, I'll allow. And I have to say your notion works, until you try to *prove* one word of it. Let's say this little lady had the motive. I know all too well what the government pays me, and it can't be paying a secretary at the BIA half that much. I can see how she'd have had the opportunity as well. Working the Osage desk, even when her boss was out of the office, surely put her in position to plot with old Bluefeather and he just proved tonight that *he* was a crook."

The older man stared down wistfully at his untasted helping of fudge cake and went on, "Bull Durham, out back, had to be in on it. But all we could prove for sure in court was that both bad boys needed some fool place to leave a gas buggy when neither was driving it. Even if we got the neighbors to say they'd ever noticed either Bluefeather or Durham one step closer to Miss Tenkiller's coffee and cake, that still wouldn't prove she was more than, say, a play-pretty either might have called on from time to time."

Helen Tenkiller blushed and snapped, "All right. If you must know I was having an affair with Walter Bluefeather, and why not? He was rich and handsome and I'm not too proud to kiss a good-looking Indian, being one myself, damn it!"

Stringer shook his head wearily and said, "Let's not worry about how well Cherokee breeds and full blood Osage might or might not admire one another, Miss Helen. You set the whole thing up as a business deal, with Bluefeather as your muscle and Bull Durham laying pipes sneaky. When your boss, Davis, got curious enough to worry any of you, you had him killed by Willy Whitehorse, the only other Indian in on the deal. When another Indian nailed your young dupe, and I was still sniffing around, you tried to make a date with me so's Bluefeather could finish me off, here. When Bull Durham spotted me sniffing even closer at the oil refinery, Bluefeather lit out after me and we all know how that turned out, don't we?"

Bill Tilghman cut in to say, "Hold on. How come Bluefeather left his gas buggy parked out back if he meant to get the drop on you over in the railroad yards, MacKail?"

Stringer looked disgusted and asked, "Would you track a man down aboard a white Buick if you didn't want it known you were still in town? Walter did get the drop on me. I was lucky. If I hadn't been, he'd have just come back here, cranked her up, and been back out on the Rocking Tipi by the time anyone got around to asking him if he'd heard I was dead."

He stared soberly at their hostess again as he added, "When Bull Durham saw the jig was up, he came back here to light out the same way. I suspected he might. So I got here first and made sure the motor wouldn't start. Before you ask me how I knew where to look for Bluefeather's horseless carriage, I knew he'd come to town with it and it wasn't parked near the refinery, Lacey's office or even near the Lacey house. That's how I knew I was right about Bluefeather not confiding everything in his lawyer. He'd never even bothered to visit his white wife."

He took another drag and went on, "When I couldn't get the Laceys to work I looked up this address in the Tulsa directory and hit the jackpot. I'm sorry about this, too, Miss Helen. For I was hoping your gracious invite might have been the start of a much more friendly relationship."

She told him again he was crazy. Bill Tilghman didn't seem to think so now, but he still said, "I dunno, Stringer. This sweet young thing surely has a lot of questions to answer when I haul her afore the grand jury. I reckon I'd better, since not another soul fits so fine as your mastermind. But what if she just hangs tough and defies us to prove it?"

Helen snapped, wild eyed, "It'll be a cold day in hell before I confess to one word of these wild charges. I'll just hold my head high and say, sure, I just love to kiss men, red and white, and sure they park out back when they come calling on me!"

Stringer just went on staring at her. So she said, defiantly, "So my boss was gunned in a saloon fight and when you questioned me at the office, I may have forgotten some of the folders we had on one or two Osage clients. What do you want to make of it, that I'm just a dumb female breed that they never should have hired to begin with?"

She turned back to Tilghman and snapped, "You just go on and arrest me, if you dare." So Tilghman nodded and said, "I mean to, Ma'am. Seeing you're fully dressed, as if you might have been planning on going somewhere tonight, in any case, we'd best all wander over to the office, now. We'll see what the federal prosecutor has to say about you making bail, if I can still get him on the telly-phone."

Tilghman got to his feet. So did Stringer. But the beautiful suspect stayed seated, insisting, "You don't have a thing on me. Not a thing that you can make stick, and you know that as well as I do."

Tilghman stared across at Stringer to say, "What am I supposed to do now, pistol whip her and drag her back to my office? I sure hate to do that, even when I got solid proof."

Stringer said, "Well, you might have, Bill. It all depends on what any good druggist can tell you about the refreshments she just served. You just commented on her being dressed as if to go out, and Bull Durham might have beat her to that Buick they both must have known about, so . . ."

"Oh my God!" Helen cut in, reaching for Stringer's untasted cup as she said, "First I'm supposed to be a master criminal and now he says I'm out to poison folk!"

Then, before either man could stop her, Helen Tenkiller had swallowed the whole cup of lukewarm coffee and leaned back in her chair with a triumphant smile, saying, "There. Do I look like I've just drunk poison?"

Bill Tilghman chuckled down at her and told Stringer, "I'd say she's got you, old son. What makes you such a suspicious cuss?"

Then, before Stringer could answer, Helen went over backwards, chair and all, and began thrashing on the floor like a snake some mean cuss had kicked into a branding fire!

As Tilghman dropped to one knee at her side he wailed, "Don't just stand there, Stringer! *Do* something!"

So Stringer ran to the sink, filled a pot with fresh water, and hunkered down on the other side of the dying girl. But she seemed to be dead before they could find out if the water might have helped or not.

As she lay dishrag limp between them, Stringer said, "It must have been something like strychnine." To which the older lawman replied, morosely, "Quicker acting than strychnine. I've seen coyotes last longer than that after swallowing such bait. I take back what I said about you being suspicious, old son. I had no idea she was that desperate."

Tilghman got slowly to his feet as he added, "She must have had a really guilty conscience, to do a fool thing like that. Had she just stuck to her guns, the odds were better than even on her walking free, you know."

Stringer got up and emptied the pot into the sink as he replied, "You heard me tell her I'd have never had call to poke into their business if they'd just left me the hell alone. But I reckon you know better than me how many folk wind up in prison, or worse, because they can't stay calm under pressure."

Bill Tilghman nodded and said, "I used to say more than half the men Judge Parker had to hang were too stupid to know which leg they was pissing down when they forgot to unbutton. You're going to have to stick around until we do the paperwork on this complexicated case, even if all the crooks seem to be dead."

Stringer nodded grimly and said, "That's all right. As long as I have two stories, now, for the price of one railroad ticket. Do you need me here any more, tonight, Bill? I thought I'd like to get back to my hotel and write some of this down while the details are still fresh in my head."

Tilghman nodded but asked Stringer to send some of the boys out back to help him tidy up the kitchen. Stringer did so and it was only a short walk back to the Osage Inn.

As he entered, he saw Irene had left, bless her, no doubt to meet her fool kid brother. He didn't care. He'd about recovered in that department, but a night alone in bed could hardly hurt him.

As he passed the desk, the night clerk called out, "Hold on, Mister MacKail," and as Stringer turned back, he saw a gal in a travel duster rising from where she'd been sitting amid lobby rubber plants. She held out her hand to Stringer, saying, "I've been waiting here in hopes of an interview, MacKail. I'm Swensen from the *Washington Post*."

As he shook with the pretty thing he noticed her hand was warm and soft as her smile and figured the back of his own neck would have felt even warmer if old Irene had been there to stare at it. This other gal didn't look all that much like a Swensen, since her hair and eyes were both soft shades of brown and she was built petite under that travel duster and perky straw boater. He said, "Pleased to meet you, pard. But don't you find it sort of unusual, interviewing other newspaper folk?"

She dimpled up at him to reply, "There's always a first time and it's not as if we worked for papers on the same coasts. The two of us seem to be covering this oil well Indian angle and while I have my own copious notes on the subject, they tell me you've been having more excitement. I think we could both file hotter stories if we put our heads together and compared coverage."

He smiled crookedly and told her, "I'd sure like to put my head next to yours Miss Swensen. But I fear my boss would have a fit. Another newspaper gal who said she was my friend just tried to scoop us on an oil well fire and . . ."

"It's out." She cut in, adding, "There's not much news in an oil well fire to begin with, unless you're watching it. The byline I'm willing to share with you is a lot bigger, and I've a fifth of I.W. Harper and three pads of shorthand at my hotel just down the street. So what do you say?"

Stringer glanced over at the desk. The clerk was pretending to read his own newspaper instead of staring right at them. So Stringer said, "That sounds more proper than inviting a lady up to my room. Lord knows I seem to have the time. I'll be stuck here in Tulsa at least a few more days. But I have to say I've been burnt more than once sharing news with members of the unfair sex. It's not that I'm greedy. But it hardly seems fair that I do all the work and you get all the details, gratis. No offense, but you just got here and they told you true when they told you I've been having an exciting time in Tulsa."

She said she was sure she could make it worth his while and then, before he could tell her she didn't look like that kind of gal, she added, "You might say I arrived with notes you couldn't have taken out here. My editor just got them from the horse's mouth before he put me on the train with orders to go get some background material to explain Teddy Roosevelt's latest outburst."

Stringer frowned down at her thoughtfully and said, "I met the president in the Yellowstone park just a spell back. I got to hunt poachers with him and Jack London. I can't recall either of 'em mentioning Tulsa or even rock-oil, though."

She nodded and said, "I just told you it was a new news item. Before I dangle some bait for you, do we have a deal?"

Stringer chuckled fondly and said, "Not hardly. I'll dangle some for you. I just now come from covering the deaths of some mighty crooked crooks who'd been robbing oil well Indians blind. Before I share note one on a story that almost got me killed I'd sure like to know what you suspect I missed."

She took his arm and led him deeper into the rubber plants as she confided, "It's too hot to let another soul in on. I know all about your recent shoot-outs. Such gossip travels fast in a town this size. All I need from you are the ways one spells all the names and such other details.

Put together with what I have, you'll be able to file a much better story and I'll admit my own copy will read better spiced with what you've found out here, on the scene. Come on. We can talk about it at my place."

Stringer could tell he'd about recovered from his earlier overindulgences with other ladies as he inhaled some of this one's musky perfume. But, trying to remember what that wise old philosopher had said about sanity, he said, "You'll have to do better than that before you lead *this* poor mortal down any primrose path, pard. You just now said I had a mighty exciting scoop of my own to keep and cherish. Do I really look dumb enough to share it with a rival paper for a belt of I.W. Harper and a hint that you might know something I don't?"

She sighed and said, "They warned me you were a hardcased pro and I can't say that lowers you in my esteem. But do I have your word you won't hold out on me if I give you all I've got?"

He raised an eyebrow at her to say, dryly, "I hardly ever hold anything out of a lady who gives me her all."

She blushed, fluttered her lashes, and said, "Don't talk fresh. We don't know one another that well, yet." Then she glanced all about, as if to make sure no other newspaper folk were lurking behind a rubber plant, and said, "All right. I'll give you the gist of it, so you can make up your mind how far you want to go with me. President Roosevelt likes to think of himself as a Westerner who admires bears, buffalo, Indians and so forth. He thought it was amusing and simple justice when we learned back East about all the rock-oil they'd discovered under land a lot of Indians had been granted at gun point, whether they wanted it or not. So when a certain senator proposed a bill that would return the civilized tribes to their original lands in the swamps and moon-shine hills east of the Mississippi, our Teddy got out his big stick and forgot what he said about speaking softly. It seems he enjoys swapping droll stories with a young part-Cherokee vaudeville star called Will Rogers and thinks the Oklahoma Indians have paid their dues twice over. So he's put his own bill before Congress, giving more property rights to any Indian who speaks English and can read and write. He says this nonsense requiring a prosperous Indian to be sponsored by even a trash white is unjust as well as silly. How do you like my own angle so far?"

Stringer chuckled and replied, "A lot better than tin-horn lawyers and Pearl Starr are likely to, if old Teddy can make it stick. The trouble with trying to grant full equality to the noble savage is that even some breeds like to feel sort of savage on the government dole. Only a very few Indians have oil wells on their property and many a trash white would take a government handout if it was offered. But you sure do raise an interesting angle and I can see how to work it in as, say, at least an extra half column."

She nodded and said, "My own feature will run longer and more interesting, once we put our heads to-gether. So why don't we just do that, MacKail?"

He thought, nodded, and they went on over to her place to get started. But once they'd shared some of that I.W. Harper after he'd seen what she looked like with her loose travel duster and dumb hat hung up beside his hat and jacket, it was tough to get started writing.

So it was a good thing, after all, that the local author-ities had asked Stringer to stick around a few days. It took close to five before the government had wrapped up the case and told him he was free to go.

If it had only taken three or four days, it seems doubtful Stringer and old Inga, as he'd learned to call her halfway down that first bottle, would ever have gotten around to putting one word down on paper.